# RETRIBUTION

JAMES MATHEW JUSTIN

INDIA • SINGAPORE • MALAYSIA

# Acknowledgements

As a first-time author, I've learned that writing a book is never a solitary journey, even when most of the work is done in silence and solitude. This story may have begun with just me and a blank page, but it would not exist without the encouragement, support, and generosity of many others.

To my family and friends, thank you for believing in me when this was nothing more than an idea and for listening patiently to countless half-formed thoughts and late-night ramblings.

To those who read early drafts, offered honest feedback, or simply asked, "How's the writing going?". Thank you. Your interest meant more than you know to me.

To my editor, who helped me shape this manuscript with care and clarity, thank you for seeing potential where I only saw pages of mess in my eyes.

And to every reader holding this book now, thank you for taking a chance on a new voice. Your time is a gift I'll never take lightly.

This is only the beginning. Welcome to Victor Harrington's world.

With heartfelt gratitude,

Yours truly,

James

* * * *

There are men who make their name in the underworld through fear and through blood. He did it through both of them.

They called him many things over the years. But only one had fitted him perfectly. The Silent Ghost. Because when he stepped into a room, the room listened.

He was the weapon the Casella family built from scratch. Adopted as a child, raised with cruelty, trained not just to kill, but to survive every kill. He didn't bleed often. And when he did, the world bled more.

Victor Harrington is the man who rose through the ranks like a curse. He fought harder, lasted longer, and thought sharper than the criminals who had centuries of blood behind them. He could break a man's spine with his legs or hands, then calmly watch the man scream in pain. He is the one who likes obtaining joy and happiness from people getting hurt. His fists are like stones. Eyes like the cold and harsh winter. A mind that remembered everything and trusted no one.

He didn't want empires. He wanted revenge on the world that made him. He saw the evil behind the power, the children trafficked, the cities gutted, the innocent sacrificed in silence. He did what no one had ever done before. Victor turned on them.

He dismantled their operations piece by piece. Ports were burned. Crime Lords were exposed. The Casella and the other empires cracked from within. He made himself a threat no syndicate could contain. A lone man who dared to wage war against the Five Pillars.

And then, just as suddenly, he disappeared. Like a ghost retreating into the fog. No trail. No sound. Only questions.

And if the underworld has learned anything over the years, it's this. Never let Victor Harrington come back to what he started or he had ended.

* * * *

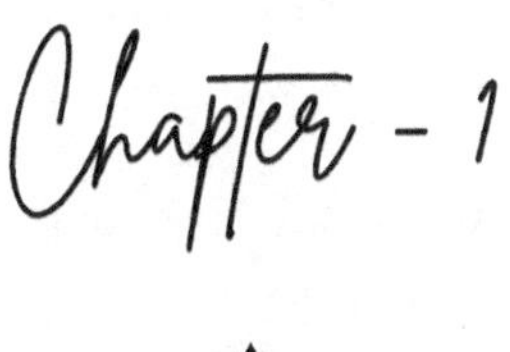

The dimly lit lobby of the Roosevelt Hotel in New York city, hummed with the quiet buzz of late-night guests. Outside, the cold New York wind rattled the glass doors. Nick Carver adjusted the collar of his worn leather jacket as he scanned the room.

David Holloway, CIA operative, leaned against the far wall, eyes sharp beneath the brim of his cap. No introductions were needed. Nick already knew why they were here.

David stepped forward, his voice low and cautious. "I've got something for you." He pulled a small USB drive from inside his coat and pressed it into Nick's hand like a fragile promise.

"As a token," David said, "for what you uncovered about the Serpent Gang's drug routes."

Nick's fingers closed around the device, the weight of it heavier than expected. "Thanks. This might be the key."

David's gaze hardened. "Listen Nick. Inside the USB are images and files about the Five Pillars. And everything you had asked. Also, there's something else." He paused, voice almost dropping to a whisper. "The Silent Ghost."

Nick's pulse quickened. The name was a legendary story whispered in the underworld—an assassin, a master of the deadly arts, but also a man with a code. Nick believed this man could be his last hope against the shadows creeping into the streets.

David's tone turned grim. "Once you open those files, they'll start deleting themselves after you close them. You get one shot. There will be no backups, no second chances."

Nick nodded slowly. "Got it."

David took a step closer, eyes scanning the surroundings. "And Nick... don't go hunting where even the CIA or anyone else won't tread. There are places so dark, even we don't want to touch them."

Nick didn't hesitate. "The deeper I research about this information, the clearer I see about it. Perhaps it was never about escaping from the mess, but understanding why I walked into it in the first place."

Nick started toward the exit, then paused. "David, what do you know about the Imperium Nexus?"

For a moment, David looked genuinely puzzled, as he looked lost. He shook his head. "Imperium what?"

Nick repeated, "Imperium Nexus. An organization. Something powerful, tied to the underworld's rise. Something beyond our understanding."

David's lips pressed into a thin line. "Never heard of it. Maybe you're chasing shadows, Nick. Just be careful. It must be an imagination. Like this Illuminati or some other brotherhood." With that, David slipped back into the room of the hotel room, leaving Nick alone with the USB and a growing storm of questions.

Outside, the city lights flickered in the rain. Nick's grip tightened around the USB. Whatever waited inside, there was no turning back now.

*     *     *     *

# Chapter - 2

Nick Carver slammed his apartment door shut behind him, breath fogging in the cold silence. The New York skyline outside his window buzzed with midnight life, but his mind was elsewhere. It was on the small USB now resting beside his laptop.

He didn't even bother to change out of his coat. Sliding into the chair, he inserted the USB. The screen flickered once, then twice. A folder appeared. "CLASSIFIED"

Nick opened it.

Files populated the screen like digital ghosts rising from the past—names, images, and documents layered with red colors, blacked-out text, and warning headers. He clicked the first one, which showed about the Five Pillars and their domains.

Five photographs appeared. Five men who were aged, grainy, yet imposing. Five crime lords. Five continents.

The first file revealed the Five Pillars. Five different crime lords ruling five continents. There was the Serpent Gang in North America, rooted in old dynasties and trafficking empires, the Red Tide in South America, warlords who ruled the drug trade.

The Casella Family in Europe, aristocratic financiers of global crime; the Saffron Group in Asia, a silent dominion hidden behind technology and espionage; and the Sahara Nexus in Africa, phantom kings dealing in diamonds and coup d'états.

Nick opened another file. He read it under his breath. "The Five Pillars were born from the chaos of World War II…"

The words sent a chill through him. He kept reading on.

In 1945, as Europe burned and empires fell, a group of war profiteers, ex-military officers, and black-market tycoons met in secret. Dividing the postwar world like territories on a game board. Each was given a continent. Each began to build a new order from the ruins. An invisible empire that outlived governments and reshaped nations.

Over the decades, they evolved. Using proxy wars, political bribes, and covert industries to tighten their grip. When the Cold War ended, the Five Pillars remained, unseen and untouched. The crime lords ruling the Five Pillars are of old bloodlines with endless wealth and deeper secrets. Their influence passed everywhere. They controlled cities without stepping into them.

And now… they were everywhere.

Nick sat back, stunned. "How deep does this go?"

Another folder pinged open without his click. It was unnamed and hidden until the rest had been accessed. The folder had a name. Valmont Industries.

Nick blinked. A sleek logo appeared. Valmont, a private defense company based in London with extensions around the urbanized areas of the world. The files were sparse, but the headlines were displayed off the screen: "Leaked Reports of Genetic Enhancement Trials." "Human Experimentation in Eastern Europe?" "Serum Code Name: Genesis."

Nick understood that these files hinted at illegal genetic experiments to enhance human abilities.

A new tab unfolded beneath it. Something named as 'The Four Horsemen.' He clicked. The screen turned black for a second before loading.

Photos emerged. Blurred faces. Bio-scans. Reports. Muscular silhouettes. Infrared combat footage. The Genesis Serum, the file said, was not for the many. Only few were chosen for this project. Few of these subjects died. But other subjects who survived gained enhanced strength, reflexes, memory, and pain tolerance. Some became nearly unkillable.

The Four Horsemen were created by Valmont industries, linked to the Five Pillars. These four people had the Genesis Serum in them.

The Maker, a genius-level strategist and the one who stays a step ahead always. The Commander, a ruthless field leader with unmatched tactical skills. The Illusionist, a master of deception and psychological techniques. And The Grim Reaper, a silent killer whose kill count spanned continents.

Nick's hands were trembling now. He leaned forward, eyes stinging. Then another image loaded. Not a file. Just a single photograph.

A man standing in a rain-soaked alley, face partly obscured by shadows. The name beneath it made Nick's heart stop cold.

Victor Harrington.

The man he'd been searching for. A ghost. A legend. A name whispered in conspiracies.

Nick's breath caught in his throat.

Victor was one of them. Or worse... the first.

Before he could process more, the files started deleting. One by one. Fast. Erased clean.

Nick yanked the USB out, but it was too late. The screen was blank. He sat there frozen, eyes wide, a cold sweat clinging to his back. Everything had changed. He knew what he wanted to know.

* * * * *

# Chapter - 3

London wore its grief well. The sky was a grim slate, heavy with clouds that wept in a quiet, persistent drizzle. Black cabs and sedans lined the narrow lanes outside Highgate Cemetery, their headlights muted by the fog that rolled in from Hampstead Heath. Crows circled the skeletal trees as if nature itself mourned alongside them.

Victor Harrington stood beneath a tall yew, his tailored overcoat soaked at the shoulders, a man carved from shadow and stone. His gloved hand clutched a white rose. The name Dante Harrington was etched into polished black granite, still pristine. His son. His blood. Now just a name in a graveyard of names. The priest's voice murmured through the rain, barely audible over the shuffle of umbrellas and quiet sobs.

Vanessa stood to his right, but she felt miles away. Her black veil masked most of her face, but Victor didn't need to see her eyes to feel the distance growing between them like a wall of ice. She held their son's childhood photo close to her chest. Dante on his sixth and his last birthday, laughing in Hyde Park, frosting on his cheeks, sunlight in his hair.

There were no bodyguards near her. No trace of their once intertwined life of protection, of mutual silence. She had come here not as Victor's wife, but as a grieving mother. And the space between them was not just physical. It was made of years of secrets, buried deals, and bloodshed Victor swore would never touch their son. And yet, here they were.

When the service ended, and the crowd began to thin out—figures in sleek coats murmuring condolences before disappearing into the rain—Vanessa remained by the grave, unmoving. Victor approached cautiously, but she didn't look at him. The umbrella above her trembled ever so slightly in her hands. "He didn't die because of fate," she said, her voice quiet and laced with fire. "He died because your past came knocking. And like always, you answered the door."

Victor said nothing. His lips pressed into a line, his eyes fixed on the carved headstone like it could somehow absorb his guilt.

"You said we were safe in London," she continued, finally turning to him. Her voice cracked. "You said the old life was over. He wasn't just our son, Victor. He was the proof we could be more than what the world made us"

Victor looked around at the damp, silent graves. London had always been a city of masks. Men in suits who ruled empires from the shadows. Backroom meetings in Mayfair. Blood spilled in basements. He had tried to leave that world. He had burned his name, hidden in plain sight under a new one.

But power, like blood, leaves a scent. "I didn't know they were watching him," Victor murmured, the words scraping from his throat. "If I had known—"

"You always knew," she interrupted. Her hand trembled now. "Don't pretend you didn't. You just hoped it wouldn't cost you anything. But it did. It cost us everything."

The silence that followed was more violent than any scream. Vanessa stepped closer to the grave and slowly placed the photograph into the earth before it was covered. "I want to remember him without guns in his future," she whispered. "Without looking over my shoulder. Without wondering which of your enemies might come for us next."

Victor reached for her hand, but she stepped back. The gesture wasn't cold, but it was final. "I'm leaving, Victor," she said softly, with the kind of calm that breaks hearts. "Not just this cemetery. Not just today. I can't be your wife anymore. I can't be the mother of your next tragedy. I hope MI6 still has a place for me. And when the storm settles, maybe I can be back for you."

Victor stood alone as she walked away, disappearing into the grey London mist with her heels echoing faintly across the wet stones. A black cab rolled up silently, its headlights cutting through the fog. She entered it without looking back. And then she was gone.

As the cab vanished into the haze, and the last echo of Vanessa's departure dissolved into the hush of rain and earth, Victor Harrington stood utterly alone. The yew tree above him creaked in the wind like an old sentinel mourning in silence.

Raindrops streaked down his cheeks, indistinguishable from tears he no longer had the strength to shed. The cold seeped into his bones, but he didn't move. Couldn't. His son's grave stood before him like a cruel mirror—still, final, and unforgiving.

And then, something inside Victor blinked.

The stillness fractured. Not with pain—but with something… off. A tickle at the back of his mind. A peculiar warmth rising behind his eyes, out of place in this bleak theatre of sorrow. Victor swayed slightly on his feet, and for a moment, the world around him dimmed. The storm clouds, the cemetery, even the grave, they all softened, lost focus. And when clarity returned, Victor Harrington was no longer there.

In his place stood a personality of a man with a strange, almost boyish brightness in his eyes. His shoulders were no longer hunched with grief, but relaxed. His lips curved into a small, playful smile. He looked around with curiosity, as though waking from a long, comfortable nap. He adjusted his collar, blinking at the gravestones as if trying to remember where he was.

"Why is everyone dressed so gloomy?" he asked softly, almost to himself, glancing down at his dark clothing like it was someone else's choice. His gaze drifted toward the fresh grave, the name etched in black granite. "Dante Harrington?" he read aloud, tilting his head. "Hmm… Doesn't ring a bell." He gave a polite shrug, his smile untouched by the name, by the weight, by the ruin it represented.

He leaned forward slightly, examining the headstone with innocent interest. "Poor fellow," he said, as if commenting on a stranger's misfortune. "I do hope he wasn't terribly sad at the end."

Then, without another glance, he turned and began to stroll away, with his hands swinging gently at his sides, the puddles splashing beneath his shoes. There was a lightness in his step, a softness in his humming, like a child walking through a garden rather than a man abandoning his son's grave.

Alexander Spector had returned with delicate kind of innocence, an echo of a shattered mind dressing its wounds in fantasy. And the world, heavy with rain and death, watched him go, unsure whether to mourn him or fear what might come next.

* * * * *

London, two years later

The morning air in Notting Hill was cool and damp, the kind that clung softly to the skin. Alexander Spector stood at his front step on Colville Terrace, a quiet street lined with pastel houses and flowering trees. He pulled his coat tighter and glanced up at the grey sky, then gently closed the door behind him. In his left hand, he held a worn leather satchel; in the right, a cup of tea from his chipped green thermos, still steaming. His steps were slow but purposeful as he made the short walk to his bookstore.

The Dust and Echo sat at the end of the lane, tucked between a flower shop and a bakery whose warm scent drifted through the air. The bookstore's faded wooden sign hung above the window, vines crawling over the frame like they were reading along with time. Inside, it was still and calm, as always. The moment Alexander unlocked the door and stepped in, he exhaled a breath he didn't realize he'd been holding.

"Good morning, old place," he said softly to the empty room, setting down his satchel. The bell above the door gave a gentle chime. He didn't turn on the overhead lights right away—just the little lamp on the counter and the string of warm fairy lights by the back shelves. It felt less lonely that way.

He moved slowly through the space, arranging the return pile, straightening a crooked poetry display, brushing dust off the top of a bookshelf. Every detail in The Dust And Echo mattered to him. The history section was alphabetized meticulously, the children's corner had beanbags and small stuffed animals tucked into the shelves. The cash register had a teacup resting beside it, which was his favorite blue-and-white ceramic one—and a stack of sticky notes scribbled with quiet thoughts or book quotes.

Alexander was soft-spoken and often avoided small talk, but when he did speak to his customers, it was always kind, sometimes shy, and often surprising in its insight. If someone asked him for a recommendation, he'd light up ever so slightly. "If you're looking for comfort," he'd say, holding out a copy of The Secret Garden, "this one always makes you feel like spring's just around the corner."

His regulars knew him well enough to not press him. They liked him for his gentleness, for how he'd smile awkwardly and offer a book as if it were a warm coat on a cold day. Children loved him too—perhaps because he listened to them like they were important. Or maybe the children treated as a source for timepass. He kept a box of old comics by the counter, and every now and then, he'd let one go for free if he saw a shy smile or tired eyes. "It's alright," he'd whisper. "Books know when they've found the right hands."

By midday, he'd brew himself a second cup of tea in the back, then sit at the tiny window table and read quietly. He favored mythology, history, and obscure nonfiction books about ancient cities. Often, he read aloud to himself in a hushed tone, not realizing he was doing it. When he stumbled over a word, he'd laugh softly and say, "Well, you're a tricky one, aren't you?"

His lunch was always the same: a sandwich wrapped in wax paper and an apple, both packed from home. Sometimes he'd pause eating to scribble in a little green notebook—ideas, memories, half-drawn maps of places he might never visit. He wrote things like: "Memory isn't a place you go back to—it's a person you carry." Or, "I think the silence speaks louder here than it ever did in the house."

The upper floor of the shop had his tiny flat. He had lived alone there. His world now was books, the quiet rain, the ticking of the old wall clock. He didn't go out much unless it was to the corner café, where they knew him by name but never asked about his past. Everyone in the neighborhood respected his distance. They saw the sadness in his eyes and gave him space.

In the evenings, he always followed the same ritual. He dusted the shelves again, even if they didn't need it. By the time he locked the shop and stepped back onto the street, the neighborhood would be wrapped in golden lamplight. He'd walk home in silence, listening to the gentle sounds of London around him—the passing cars, the distant laughter, the rustling of trees.

And once he was home, he would sit in the same chair by the window, drink one last cup of tea, and let the soft sound of the radio play old jazz records until sleep overtook him.

Alexander didn't speak much of the past anymore. Not even to himself. But in the quiet, in the pages of forgotten books, in the soft corners of the shop, his grief lived gently, like a story waiting to be understood.

* * * * *

# Chapter - 5

Alexander woke with the heavy stillness of morning wrapped around him like a fog. His apartment on Colville Terrace remained as it always did, always small, cozy, filled with books and warmth, but something in the air felt displaced, as though a piece of it had shifted in the night when he wasn't looking.

He sat up on the edge of the bed, staring down at his slippers. The blanket was crumpled and tossed to the floor, and the curtains, which were usually drawn halfway, were wide open. He never left them open. Alexander was, if nothing else, a man of gentle routines. Tea at eight-thirty, bookstore doors open by nine-fifteen and jazz on vinyl at seven in the evening, and bed with a book by eleven sharp. These patterns were his quiet map through the day.

And yet lately, things had begun to happen. Small things, but strange. Two nights ago, he'd woken in the hallway, standing barefoot on the cold floorboards. The hallway lamp had been unscrewed, the bulb placed neatly on the table. Last night, he had gone to bed wearing flannel pajamas. He awoke in a black turtleneck he didn't remember owning.

He blinked now at the sunlight streaking in through the windows. A small voice in his mind murmured, "Get up, Alexander. The day waits for no one."

His head snapped to the side. The voice had sounded like his. Almost. Except it hadn't. It was lower, smoother. There was a faint lilt to the vowels. An accent. British, he thought, almost imperceptible but there. Elegant, stern. Familiar and foreign.

He stood slowly, brushing off a chill that didn't belong to the room.

After breakfast, which consisted of toast and orange marmalade, he walked to his bookstore. The bell above the door gave its usual warm chime as he stepped inside. He inhaled the smell of pages and old wood. Here, everything still made sense.

The regulars came and went. Mrs. Elkins for her garden books, Peter from the café picking up another copy of Orwell's essays. Alexander helped out a shy university student find an out-of-print poetry collection, wrapping it carefully in brown paper and string. All the while, the day passed like silk. Almost normal.

But when he went into the backroom to fetch inventory, the air felt different. Not colder, but denser. A strange scent lingered in the air, like sandalwood and dust.

And then, again, the voice came. "Words are your armor. But they won't stop the war that's coming., Alexander."

Alexander dropped the book in his hands. He spun around. The room was empty. "Hello?" he called gently, his voice thin and disbelieving. The light buzzed overhead. No one answered.

He knelt to pick up the book and noticed his hands were trembling. He swallowed hard and forced a breath out, half-laughing under it. "Probably the flu," he whispered to himself. "Or lack of sleep. Too much of tea I guess."

That night, he sat in bed with a book open on his lap, unread. His eyes flicked to the door, then to the clock. Midnight. Outside, the street was quiet. The voice hadn't returned all evening. Maybe it had been a one-off. A dream layered onto wakefulness.

He turned off the light and lay back. The quiet of the room pressed around him, like soft velvet. He drifted to sleeping.

And then, something cold brushed him. A whisper which was not from the room, but from inside his skull. "You don't know what you're capable of, Alexander. But I do."

His eyes opened wide. He sat up fast. The lamp flicked on without his hand touching it. He stared at the empty room. "No," he said aloud, his voice breaking. "I—I don't understand."

The voice, which sounded exactly like his, came again, this time slower, closer. "Of course you don't. You're not meant to. You were made to forget."

Alexander stumbled out of bed, heart pounding. He opened his closet—just to check. Empty. He stepped into the hallway, calling softly, "Is anyone there?" He knew there wasn't. But something in him needed confirmation. The air held its silence like a held breath.

Later, as dawn broke through the curtains, he sat in the kitchen, unable to sleep. The teacup in his hand rattled against the saucer. His journal lay open on the table. A single line, written in ink he did not remember using.

"You are not alone. I am always here."

He ran his fingers over the handwriting. It was his, and not his. More elegant. Slanted. Foreign.

"I think I'm bloody mad," he whispered, voice barely audible over the ticking clock.

But even as he said it, the other voice laughed gently in the back of his mind. "No, Alexander. You're not mad. You're waking up. Let me out."

And Alexander, gentle and unsure, sat in the glow of morning, too polite to argue with the voice inside his own head.

* * * * *

# Chapter - 6

It was just past noon when a thin drizzle began to darken the brick sidewalks of Notting Hill. The chiming bells above the glass door of the bookstore had gone quiet for nearly an hour, leaving Alexander alone among the whispers of books and the gentle hum of classical music playing from an old turntable behind the counter. He was mid-shelving a stack of antique philosophy texts, humming softly to himself, when the postman arrived with a smile and the day's newspaper.

"Thank you, mate." Alexander said with his usual soft tone, giving a polite nod as he accepted the bundle of letters and the neatly folded edition of The Times.

He set the stack on the counter and returned to the shelf. But something on the front page caught his eye, a bold print framed by black ink.

"Casella Brothers Elude Capture Again: Carabinieri Frustrated by Lack of Progress, Organized Crime Syndicate Expands Influence Across Europe"

Alexander slowly reached for the paper. The name struck him, not with familiarity, but with an eerie sense of displacement. Casella. It rang in his head like a name spoken long ago in a life forgotten. He stared at the article, reading slowly.

For over a decade, the Casella family—led by the infamous two brothers, Giovanni and Leonardo Casella—has run one of the most powerful criminal organizations in Europe. Despite several international operations coordinated by the Carabinieri, MI6 and Interpol, the Casella brothers remain at large. Their empire stretches throughout the entire continent of Europe, with rumors of past political ties and underground financial networks still under investigation.

Alexander whispered the name again under his breath. "Casella..." Something about it pulled at him. But no memory followed, only silence. Alexander set the paper down as if it had burned his fingers. "Nothing much, mate. Just the imagination," he muttered, brushing his palm against his temple. But a faint unease pressed into him like a shadow stretching across the floor.

As he tried to return to sorting books, the door chimed again.

In walked a woman with a navy trench coat and black boots, carrying a closed umbrella and a warm, knowing smile. She had thick auburn hair tied into a low bun and eyes that sparkled with a mix of familiarity and charm. She didn't hesitate as she walked directly up to the counter.

"Alexander," she said with a charming look, "I just wanted to remind you our dinner's tomorrow at seven, not tonight. Lucca's—you remember?"

He blinked, utterly lost. "Dinner?"

Her brows lifted slightly. "You didn't forget, did you?" Her tone was amused, not accusatory.

There was a pause. Alexander smiled, though there was a flicker of confusion behind it. "Ah. Right. Lucca's. Tomorrow evening. Yes, of course."

She studied him for a moment, then laughed lightly. "You've got too many dusty old books in your head. Don't overthink it. I'll meet you there."

Alexander offered a soft chuckle. "Looking forward to it, Elena."

She touched the edge of the counter briefly with her fingertips before turning toward the door. "Take care, book man."

As she disappeared down the street and into the rain, Alexander stood motionless for a moment. Elena was next door his neighbor. He remembered now. Third floor, just across the hall. Always friendly. He remembered a short conversation about their favorite authors, a joke she'd made about him living in his bookstore more than his flat.

But dinner? Had he really arranged it?

And that voice again, just at the edge of thought, slipping between the cracks: "You'll remember. Sooner or later."

Alexander pressed a hand against the counter to steady himself. The bookstore felt colder suddenly, though the heaters buzzed quietly under the window. He reached for the newspaper again, heart beating slower now, but heavier. The Casella name sat there like a weight. A name that meant nothing. And yet everything.

Outside, the rain whispered down. Inside, the shop was quiet. But Alexander no longer felt alone.

* * * * *

# Chapter – 7

The soft hum of conversation, the gentle clinking of cutlery, and the warm scent of garlic and roasted tomatoes gave Luca's its usual inviting glow. Tucked into the corner of Pembridge Road, the small Italian place always felt suspended in time, with its black-and-white photos of old Naples and strings of amber bulbs hanging like tired fireflies.

Alexander arrived early, five minutes, or maybe more. He had taken time getting dressed: a navy blazer, freshly ironed white shirt, polished brown shoes he hadn't worn in years. They felt foreign, stiff, like artifacts from a life that didn't quite belong to him anymore. Still, he smiled politely at the waiter and asked for a table by the window. He sat down, checked his watch, and folded his hands in his lap.

Seven o'clock came and went. The waiter passed by once, then twice, offering water, then bread. Alexander declined the wine menu. "Just waiting for someone," he said with a thin smile.

By seven-fifteen, he checked his phone. A quick message sent. No reply. By seven-thirty, he sent another.

Still nothing. At seven forty-five, he called. Straight to voicemail.

The restaurant around him carried on: laughter, the scrape of plates, soft violin music drifting from overhead speakers. But his table felt separate, it felt like an island, which was somewhat quiet and apart.

His palms were damp. He loosened his collar. The breadbasket sat untouched in front of him. He stared through the window, watching headlights blur through the misted glass. Every time the door opened, his head turned, a hope in him flickering, then fading. Again. And again.

By eight, he stopped pretending she might still walk through the door. He leaned forward, elbows on the table, pressing his fingers to his temples. His chest felt tight— not from embarrassment, not even from anger, but from that slow, familiar collapse. That hollowness that had been following him lately, whispering doubts. A quiet voice, always just beneath the surface.

He couldn't shake the thought: She's not coming. She didn't forget. She chose not to.

He stood slowly, the legs of the chair scraping softly against the tiled floor. He left a few bills on the table, enough to cover the unused setting. He didn't say goodbye to the waiter. Outside, the cold hit him sharp in the face.

He walked a few steps down Pembridge Road and stopped. He took out his phone and looked at the last message again. "Looking forward to seeing you." It sat there like a stone.

Then the voice came, quiet, familiar, too close. "You thought you could keep me quiet. But you're slipping, Alexander."

His breath caught. He blinked hard, gripping the phone tighter. That voice again. His own voice, but distant, fractured. As if something else had borrowed it.

He turned around slowly, scanning the quiet street. No one. Nothing. Just the soft rumble of traffic in the distance and the echo of a violin drifting faintly from the restaurant behind him.

His hand trembled.

* * * * *

A lexander's eyes opened without warning.

The room was quiet, steeped in darkness, but not the restful kind. His chest rose and fell with strange rhythm, as if his body had been waiting—primed—for something. The soft creak of floorboards beneath him registered faintly, though he hadn't moved yet. There was no sound, no dream, no fear. Just a blank pull that seemed to rise from within his ribs and guide him like a current.

Alexander sat up in bed, his face unreadable, muscles stiff. The walls of his bedroom loomed like strangers around him. He rubbed at his eyes, but the fog didn't clear. Something was off. He could feel it in the silence. In his limbs. In the dull, inexplicable ache behind his eyes.

Then, with a stillness that felt almost mechanical, Alexander stood and walked across the room. His feet moved before thought could form. He reached the old wooden cupboard he rarely touched—its edges hidden in the shadows. His hand went straight to a panel beneath, pressing it like muscle memory. A click sounded. Then another. The compartment opened, revealing a hidden drawer inside. A box lay there, smooth, aged, wooden.

He stared at it with a blank, faraway expression. Then he opened it.

Two compact handguns lay in a black cloth, spotless. He didn't blink. His hands moved again—slow, practiced. He picked them up, checked their chambers, tucked them beneath his coat. There was no fear in him. No hesitation. Just a dull surge of cold readiness, the kind that came from someplace buried deep.

He descended the staircase slowly, like descending into water. The house offered no protest. Even the usual ticking of the old hallway clock seemed to have paused.

The night was colder than expected. His breath curled out in visible spirals as he stepped onto the damp street. The pavement gleamed under the glow of distant streetlamps. The world was quiet, not asleep but paused—like something was watching.

As he turned a corner, Alexander spotted movement in the distance. A group of figures. Dark clothes. Quick hands working on a locked side gate. Thieves. He didn't know how he knew—they simply were. Without a word, his pace quickened. His fists tightened.

The first man turned just as Alexander reached him. No words. Just motion.

Alexander struck with a viciousness that even he didn't see coming. The impact was precise, brutal—his hand moving before thought caught up. The man dropped. Another lunged. Alexander twisted the attacker's arm, slammed him against a wall. The sound of a grunt, a rib cracking. The third pulled something sharp—Alexander ducked, then elbowed the figure with such force that they collapsed onto the concrete, gasping.

His breath was now ragged. His arms burned. His vision blurred at the edges. He could hear his own heartbeat in his ears, impossibly loud, as if the world was caving in around him. His hands were shaking, blood pounding too hard. The surge of adrenaline had crested, and now it was crashing.

Alexander staggered back a step. His knees buckled. Everything tilted—sky, pavement, shadow—twisting violently as his body finally gave in. The rush, the rage, the focus—it had all been too much. He collapsed to the ground, his vision flickering like a dying lightbulb. For a split second, he saw his reflection in a darkened window.

He didn't recognize himself. Then the world went black.

* * * * *

He was back in bed, lying stiffly under the covers, cold sweat dried on his neck. The ceiling looked wrong somehow. Or maybe it was just his eyes. He sat up slowly, pain blooming in his shoulders, his arms sore. His hands bore red marks—bruised knuckles, scraped skin. His breath caught.

He had no memory of how he got here.

Alexander stared at his own reflection in the mirror beside his wardrobe. For several seconds, he simply looked. Then he whispered, "Did I... do something?"

No answer. No noise. Just silence—and the deepening fear that something inside him was slipping out when he wasn't looking.

* * * *

# Chapter - 9

The sky was dull grey by the time Alexander left his house at morning, his scarf loosely wrapped, coat tugged high on his neck. The air tasted of mist and cold metal, and the streets were still wet from a light drizzle that had passed in the early hours. He had managed to sleep a little longer than usual, though the remnants of his dream—or whatever it was—still clung to him like damp cloth.

His legs carried him through the quiet lanes, past shuttered bakeries and the occasional cyclist. Yet even as he walked, something itched at the back of his mind. He paused once near a crosswalk and glanced behind him casually. A man and woman—both sharply dressed, in dark clothes—turned away just as his eyes met theirs.

It might have been nothing. Or it might have. He didn't stop again until he reached the bookstore.

Inside, the scent of parchment and wood polish embraced him like an old friend. Dust glinted in the filtered morning light streaming through the large windows. Without speaking to himself, he removed his coat, hung it on the rack, and began sorting the new arrivals on the counter. Fiction, memoir, poetry, and the odd translated manuscript that likely hadn't sold in years. The bookstore was normal and quiet. The way he liked it.

He was halfway through rearranging a display on London authors when the bell above the door rang. A woman stepped in, her heels tapping softly across the wooden floor. Alexander looked up briefly, prepared to offer his usual kind nod and greeting, but paused.

She looked right at him. Not at the books. Not around the room. Directly at him, with a familiarity that made his spine stiffen. "Victor?" she said softly, as if confirming a name she hadn't said in years.

He blinked. His hand remained frozen on a copy of Atonement. "I'm sorry?"

She tilted her head, confusion washing over her elegant face. "It's me... Vanessa."

He furrowed his brows, lowering the book. "I think you may have the wrong person."

Her eyes didn't move. "You don't recognize me?"

"No," he said, and the answer came too fast, too flat.

The woman, who called herself as Vanessa, took a step closer. "Victor Harrington. I am your wife, you've been gone for almost a year." Her voice trembled with something deeper than surprise. "And now you're here, pretending to be someone else? I know I am sorry for leaving you like that, but times change."

"I'm not pretending anything," he replied, suddenly aware of how dry his mouth felt. "My name is Alexander. Alexander Spector. I've lived here nearly two years."

Vanessa's eyes filled with disbelief. "This isn't possible. I've looked everywhere... You vanished after—" She stopped herself, voice cracking slightly. "I know what happened to our son. It's all tied to the Five Pillars and the Saffron Group."

Alexander took a step back, a tremor in his hands now. "I'm sorry... I truly don't know you."

For a moment, they stood in silence. The only sound was the faint shuffle of paper from the open book on the counter.

Vanessa's voice dropped lower. "You don't remember anything? Not even me?"

"Sometimes I... forget things." Alexander had admitted quietly. "But this isn't a face I'd forget."

Her expression shifted. Not anger, not grief, but a quiet, awful pity. "I think," she said gently, "you've forgotten more than you realize." She looked around once more, almost taking in the books, then turned toward the door. "I'll be back soon. Let me get the car."

Then she was gone.

Alexander remained frozen behind the counter. His hand brushed over the book he'd dropped—The Remains of the Day. The title suddenly felt heavier than it should have.

He whispered under his breath, "Victor Harrington...?"

But the name sparked nothing real, but only a silence that now seemed heavier than ever before.

*  *  *  *

# Chapter – 10

The living room was still, peaceful—the kind of calm he'd grown to appreciate. On the small television mounted opposite of him, was the morning news which had droned softly, and a background noise to a mind already swirling with half-memories and unanswered questions.

Then the headline changed.

"Breaking news this morning," the anchor announced, her voice sharpening as the screen transitioned to grainy footage. "Scotland Yard confirms that the elusive international fugitive, Victor Harrington, was allegedly spotted at a bank in Notting Hill late last night. The man, believed to be responsible for multiple high-profile assassinations, organized mercenary operations, and key involvement in gang-related conflicts across Europe, remains at large. Authorities are warning citizens to stay vigilant and report any suspicious behavior, if the accused is near you or if you spot him."

Alexander's brow furrowed. The camera cut to blurry CCTV stills, just vague enough to be doubted, but clear enough that something clenched inside him. The man on the screen had his posture. His frame. His coat. That was him.

He stared at it in silence. The name, Victor Harrington had sent an odd tremor through his chest. It wasn't familiar. And yet, it rang inside his skull like a bell buried under water. Distant, muffled, but heavy.

He blinked slowly, confusion settling in his gut like wet cement. "Who the hell is Victor Harrington?" he whispered aloud, placing the coffee mug down on the table with a shaky hand.

Then, the voice returned. Not like a thought or like a whisper. But a real voice, lodged in his mind and humming low in his ears. Clear, measured and calm. And this time, without the faint accent that once haunted his other episodes. It was completely him.

"I am," the voice said.

Alexander froze. His breath hitched, heart thudding hard against his ribs. The air felt heavier now, and the familiar warmth of his flat turned colder around the edges. "What?" he said, eyes narrowing as he stood slowly. "Who are you?"

"You've always known," the voice continued, quiet but firm. "You just chose to forget. But I didn't. I remembered everything for us."

He stumbled back against the couch, the room tilting ever so slightly. His hands gripped the armrest like a man clinging to a cliff's edge. "That doesn't make sense. I don't know you. I don't know any of this," he said aloud, his voice cracking with disbelief. "I'm not—this isn't real."

"It is. And soon, you'll remember why."

There was silence again. The voice vanished as quickly as it had come, leaving only the hum of the TV and the shallow breaths of a man teetering on the edge of two lives. Alexander's gaze dropped to his trembling hands, and the last words from the news anchor repeated themselves in his head like a siren. "Victor Harrington remains at large."

He looked again at the face on the television. His own face. A ghost of himself, moving through the shadows of a life he didn't even know he had.

And for the first time since the blackouts began, months ago, Alexander felt truly afraid.

* * * * *

# Chapter – 11

Alexander rubbed his temple slowly. Sleep had been scattered for days. More blackouts. More strange gaps in time he couldn't explain. The growing pile of unaccounted hours had become too hard to ignore. Waking up with his bedsheets tangled in odd ways, bruises on his knuckles, clothes out of place. But today, there a growing pressure inside him. Something was pressing against the surface of his thoughts, like a tide rising.

Then it came. The voice. Crisp. Calm. Confident.

"You're not losing your mind, Alexander."

He froze. His spine stiffened, and his hands gripped the edge of the counter. The voice had come from nowhere, and yet it echoed with such clarity that it felt like someone had whispered it into his ear. But no one was there. No one had entered. He was still alone.

His breath caught. "Who said that?"

"I did. And so did you."

The words came gently, but carried weight. They weren't the internal ramblings of stress or exhaustion. The voice was undeniably his, and yet, in some way, not. It was smoother, deeper, tinged with something unfamiliar. A tone of certainty and power. It didn't have the hesitancy that lived in Alexander's own voice. And for a moment, he couldn't breathe.

"This isn't real," he whispered, stepping around the counter, eyes scanning the shop. Shelves stood tall and still. No movement. No shadow. No footsteps. Just the scent of parchment and old wood.

"You've felt it, haven't you?" the voice asked. "The hours missing. The sleep that doesn't rest you. The bruises you don't remember earning."

"I'm tired," Alexander murmured to himself, gripping a nearby shelf to steady himself. "That's all. I've just been tired lately."

"Tired of what, though? Of pretending this life is enough? Of trying to forget who you were?"

He backed up slowly, shaking his head. "I run a bookstore. I live a quiet life. I don't know what you're talking about."

"You used to. But the world hasn't forgotten you, Alexander. Even if you've buried yourself in fiction and dust."

He sat down heavily on the armchair near the reading nook, chest heaving now. He ran his hands through his hair, fingers trembling slightly. "What is this? Who are you?"

"I am you," came the answer. "A version you locked away. A name you scrubbed clean."

Silence followed, heavy and pulsing. He shut his eyes for a second, the inside of his head ringing like a struck bell. And then, almost like lightning in his mind, images flickered.

A woman's voice, warm and firm. A child's laughter, a brief, echoing like a memory nearly erased. The slam of a car door. Running footsteps. The feel of a cold gun handle in his hand. Screaming. A burning house. Smoke and ash.

Alexander gasped, hand over his mouth. "What was that?"

"You remember her," the voice said. "Vanessa. Our wife. And the boy, Dante."

His blood ran cold at the names. He didn't recognize them consciously, but deep down, they sparked something raw. Pain. Real, thunderous pain. "I don't know them," he whispered. "I don't know them…"

"You don't want to. But it's all coming back." Then, the voice shifted. It softened, but carried a deeper authority now. "My name… is Victor. Victor Harrington."

The name hit him like a gut punch. He curled slightly into himself, palms pressing into his temples. That name, it had appeared in the news. It had lived in the corners of his blackouts, in the mirror glances he avoided. He had seen it. That name was associated with crimes, syndicates, operations across Europe.

"That's not me," he murmured. "I'm not a killer."

"Not anymore," Victor replied. "But I was. And so were you, once."

Alexander looked up slowly, staring at his own reflection in the front window. The fading dusk outside made it faint, but there he was—eyes wide, haunted, lost. "What do you want from me?"

"To prepare," the voice answered. "She's coming back. Vanessa. You'll need me when she does. She needs us, for getting back on Dante's death."

The ticking of the wall clock was the only reply for a long time. Outside, London carried on like nothing had changed.

* * * * *

# Chapter - 12

The silence inside the bookstore was thin, like a sheet of glass waiting to crack. Alexander stood behind the counter, eyes unfocused, pretending to read while his thoughts tangled around each other. The conversation with the Victor still echoed like a storm fading into mist. His hands were calm now, but inside, something restless shifted beneath his skin. He hadn't told anyone. Who would believe him? A voice, inside his head, claiming a name that didn't belong to him.

He sighed, rubbing his temple. Then came a sound that didn't fit the quiet world he had built around himself.

A low, purring engine, smooth and expensive, slid into the street like a black panther. He looked through the window and saw the sleek body of an Aston Martin Vanquish glide to a stop. The door swung open.

She stepped out. Vanessa.

Her presence was magnetic. Tall, composed, dressed in a sharp black coat that fluttered slightly in the breeze. Her heels clicked confidently against the pavement as she crossed toward the shop without hesitation, like a woman with a mission.

Alexander didn't even have time to process it before the door swung open, the little bell ringing overhead, and her palm came crashing against his cheek.

The slap stung through skin and bone, snapping his head sideways. He staggered, blinking. For a second, the world was static. Then it began to tilt. Just like before. A shift in breath. A pull in his chest.

And the smirk curled onto his lips like an old reflex. Victor opened his eyes. He straightened his back and rolled his shoulder. "That's certainly one way to say hello."

Vanessa's arms were folded, but there was fire in her eyes. "It's been over a year." Victor tilted his head. "You look good."

"You don't," she snapped.

He chuckled softly, rubbing his cheek. "Still got that fire, huh?"

There was silence between them for a second, a silence that carried memory, which had shared nights, bloody missions, moments between fights, and goodbyes that never quite lasted. Her gaze softened a little, though her posture stayed firm.

"I should've known," she muttered. "The way you vanished. You always ran when things got too real."

"Maybe I ran to stay alive," Victor replied, voice lower now. "Maybe I forgot who I was. Also, it was you who told me to leave you alone."

She stepped closer, then handed him a key. "You remember how to drive?"

He took it with a small grin. "Only faster than anyone you know."

Outside, the Aston Martin waited like a beast on a leash. Victor opened the door for her and then slid into the driver's seat. The engine roared to life, deep and elegant. As they pulled away from the curb, Vanessa glanced at him.

"You know they spotted you."

He kept his eyes on the road. "Figured it out. It was a messy night."

"You were seen at a bank. Security footage went global. MI6 picked it up this morning. You wiped out a group of armed men in under three minutes."

"Did I?" he muttered. "Funny. I barely remember the night."

She turned away, watching the buildings blur past. "That's why I came. I had to know if it was really you... or just the ghost of you."

"And now that you know?"

Vanessa was quiet for a second. Then she reached over and placed her hand over his on the gear shift.

"I missed you, Victor. Even the damaged, forgetful version of you."

His hand turned over, wrapping gently around hers. "I missed you too."

They drove on in silence for a while, the city lights bleeding onto the windshield. He remembered every street they passed, even though part of him didn't feel like he'd been here in years. It was like waking up from a long sleep and finding the world unchanged—but you no longer recognized your own face.

Then Vanessa spoke again. "I found something."

His grip on the wheel tightened slightly. "Go on."

"A name and a location. Someone linked to Dante's death."

Victor's throat went dry. "Not speculation?" he asked. "Something real?"

She nodded. "He was seen in London. Sloppy, like he thought no one was looking anymore. But I've tracked enough of these bastards to know when the trail is fresh."

Victor didn't say anything. He slammed his foot on the accelerator. The engine screamed forward, slicing through the London roads. His face was stone, his eyes locked ahead like a missile that had found its target.

Vanessa held onto the edge of her seat, watching him. "You're not the only one who wants justice," she said.

Victor didn't blink. "I don't want justice."

He looked at her, eyes darker now, older. "I want the truth. Then I want to murder the people who took my boy. All of them."

* * * * *

# Chapter – 13

"I figured we could use a proper place to breathe," he said lightly.

She glanced at the towering structure, then at him, skeptical but silent. Inside, the two were ushered to a suite on the upper floors, all velvet finishes and muted lighting. The windows gave a sweeping view of the city skyline that felt distant.

Victor unbuttoned his coat, shrugging it off as he walked into the washroom, stripping off the remnants of the drive and its emotions. The water hit his face like a slap of clarity, cold but necessary. After a few minutes, he emerged, towel around his neck, hair damp, and expression calmer. He pulled on a crisp white shirt, rolled the sleeves, adjusted his watch—and froze.

His head dipped slightly. There was a flicker. A twist behind the eyes.

"You smug idiot." Alexander's voice snapped from within. Victor's hand trembled slightly at the cuff. "You took everything. My life. My peace. My mind."

Victor closed his eyes, exhaling slowly. "I didn't choose this either," he muttered to himself, not knowing if he was whispering or thinking. "I didn't ask for the world to bury us."

"You didn't fight it either," Alexander hissed. "I was happy. I had control. And now I'm watching you taking control of the body."

The bathroom door creaked open. Vanessa stepped into the hallway, pausing when she saw him, half-dressed, fists clenched at his sides, his back to her. Her voice cut through the tension.

"Victor... you alright?"

He blinked. The voice inside recoiled but didn't leave. "Yeah," he said without turning. "Just... memories."

Vanessa crossed her arms slowly. "No. That wasn't just a memory. You were arguing. I could hear it."

Victor looked at her over his shoulder, managing a tired smirk. "Talking to ghosts, I guess."

She didn't laugh. "You're not well, are you?"

"Who is, these days?"

He buttoned the shirt and reached for his jacket. "Come on. You said your contact wouldn't wait forever."

Vanessa let it drop, but only just. They left the hotel quietly. The Mayfair air had a winter bite to it as they moved through the quieter streets of central London. She led them toward an industrial block tucked near the river—formerly abandoned, now repurposed for operations that never saw daylight.

A row of warehouses stood in silence. Victor followed her across the cracked pavement to a rusted side door. She tapped a code on a panel concealed beneath an old vent. The door clicked open.

Inside, the safehouse was sparse but functional. There were steel chairs, bare lighting, and a long table with old dossiers and surveillance images spread across it. On the far side of the room sat a man in his forties, hunched over a folder, chain-smoking.

"That's him," Vanessa whispered. "His name's Carlo. Logistics man for the Casellas. Been with the Casella family since the old Naples days. He was close to Dante. Loyal, until they betrayed him too."

Victor stepped forward. "He knows we're coming?"

"Not exactly," she said. "But he knows something. About the night Dante died."

As they approached, Carlo looked up. His eyes widened at the sight of Victor. He stood, mouth slightly open. "You..." Carlo breathed. "You're not supposed to be alive."

Victor's jaw clenched. The shadows behind his eyes flickered again, and somewhere deep inside, Alexander stirred.

* * * * *

# Chapter – 14

The door hadn't even creaked closed behind them when Carlo shifted in his seat. He pressed something beneath the table, a faint click that Victor heard too late. Outside, boots shuffled. Shadows passed the slatted windows. Vanessa's hand slid instinctively toward her concealed holster. Victor's jaw tightened.

From every angle, doors, windows, upper vents, men began flooding in. Black gear, face masks, Casella standard-issue weapons. Silent, swift, merciless. They were surrounded.

Carlo stood now, his calm gone. "You should have stayed dead," he said, voice sharp and bitter. "You betrayed the family. Walked out with the woman. Left it all behind like you weren't born in the blood."

Victor's eyes narrowed. "I buried my name the night they turned on me."

Carlo scoffed. He leaned in slightly, voice dropping to a razor-sharp whisper. "You were never out of the game, Victor. We simply paused your chapter. Now it's time for the Five Pillars to write the ending."

Before the next breath, Victor lunged forward. His fist collided with Carlo's jaw, sending him stumbling into the wall. A sharp command was told by one of the mercs. The room erupted. Vanessa dove behind a metal crate, Victor taking cover beside her. The crates split under bullets as the room turned into chaos.

"Victor," Vanessa shouted, tossing him a second gun. "Dance with me."

His smirk was wild. "Thought you'd never ask."

Together they moved like memory. Fluid, brutal and coordinated. Victor swept low, disarming one mercenary and turning his own weapon against him. Vanessa spun, ducking, firing, every shot deliberate. The two cut through the chaos which was unstoppable in rage.

Carlo made a run for the back, limping toward the service exit. Vanessa spotted him. "He's running!"

Victor broke formation, bolting after him. In the narrow corridor behind the safehouse, he caught Carlo mid-sprint, slamming him against the concrete wall. His hands locked around Carlo's throat.

"Who gave the order?" he roared, eyes blazing.

"I don't take orders—" Carlo wheezed, but Victor wasn't hearing it.

"You watched him die!" Victor's voice cracked with fury. "You let them kill him like nothing!"

He raised his arm, ready to end it. But in the blur of rage, something shifted inside. A deep inhale. The muscles in his arm stopped moving. The hand trembled. And then came silence.

"Stop," said a calmer voice. British, measured, frightened. Alexander. His hands dropped. Carlo gasped for air, sliding to the floor. Vanessa rounded the corner, weapon raised. She caught the flicker in Victor's eyes.

"Alexander?" she asked, uncertain.

He turned to her, blinking, disoriented. "Vanessa… sorry. I—I didn't mean to… I didn't want to do it."

A sharp bang snapped through the hallway. Vanessa had shot Carlo clean through the leg, sending him sprawling.

"Talk," she growled, now pointing the gun at his forehead. "Give me the name. Who killed Dante?"

Carlo whimpered, trying to crawl back. Blood pooled beneath him. "You have no idea what you're touching. You're hunting ghosts in a burning house…"

Vanessa cocked the gun louder.

Carlo's breathing grew shallow. "It was the Grim Reaper. He was sent by the Casella brothers. Victor ruined the business. Took their ports, exposed their money laundering ops, sent their leader to prison. This was their payback."

Vanessa didn't blink. But she saw Alexander—detached, looking at the concrete wall like it was breathing.

"And if you think you can just take on one syndicate," Carlo rasped, "you better know this—the other four will come for you. For your husband. The Five Pillars don't forgive, but they erase."

A heartbeat passed.

Then a final shot rang out. Carlo slumped, lifeless. Vanessa lowered her gun, breathing fast, then grabbed Alexander's arm. "We're done here." She dragged him out through the back alley, their shadows cutting across the orange-lit street.

Only when they reached the car did she stop, her eyes not leaving him.

"You're not right," she said. "Something's wrong with you, Victor. Or Alexander. Or whoever the hell I'm talking to."

Alexander didn't answer.

* * * *

# Chapter - 15

The weight of Carlo's words still echoed in the car, as if the engine was struggling to carry it. The Five Pillars. The Grim Reaper. A life Victor once buried clawing its way back from the shadows. And Alexander, caught between it all, was fraying. They didn't speak much as they left the warehouse.

Halfway down the empty road, headlights carving through the London mist, Alexander shifted in the passenger seat. "I can't do this," he muttered.

Vanessa glanced sideways, her hands firm on the wheel.

"This is too much," he said, his voice trembling. "Gunfire, crime, secrets, people dying. I didn't ask for this... I don't even know who I am anymore."

She didn't interrupt.

"I thought I was just a man with a quiet life and a bookshop... but it turns out I'm someone else. Someone everyone fears. Someone with a past full of violence. I can't carry that weight, Vanessa. Not now."

A breath passed. Then a stillness. Victor stirred from the back of his mind, like a storm waiting to crash.

Alexander exhaled. "He wants to come back. I'll let him. I just... need to step away."

His voice dropped to a whisper. "Tell him... not to get us killed."

Vanessa nodded slightly. "I'll try."

Then, in the next moment, his posture changed. Eyes sharpening. Shoulders settling back like muscle memory had taken the wheel. It wasn't Alexander anymore.

Victor was back. He flexed his fingers slightly, rolled his neck, and looked out the window like it was all familiar again. "I used to hate riding shotgun," he muttered.

Vanessa grinned faintly, but it didn't reach her eyes. "And I used to think you'd grow up one day."

Victor smirked. "Still waiting?"

"No," she replied flatly. "I just expect your habits to eventually kill us both."

She turned off the main road, gliding into the private entrance of a luxury hotel tucked between two towering banks. Victor scanned the exterior—glass façade, discreet cameras, and no one loitering outside. Just the kind of place he'd have picked back when he had empires chasing him.

They checked in without words. The room on the top floor was quiet, too pristine. It smelled like money and forgotten promises.

Inside, Victor dropped onto the bed without even taking off his boots.

Vanessa stood by the window, her hands resting on the glass as she watched the cars passing below. Her reflection looked hollow, tired, fractured. Like she was staring at a version of herself she hadn't spoken to in months.

"I'll be back in a minute," she said without turning around. "I need some air."

Victor gave a soft grunt. Not an answer, not resistance.

The door clicked shut behind her.

Victor lay motionless, staring up at the ceiling. He had returned back to the underworld. Sleep tugged at his mind like a slow current, and his eyes drifted shut. But real sleep? That was harder to find these days.

* * * * *

There was no beginning to the darkness in his dream. No horizon, no floor beneath his feet, but only an endless void that breathed with a slow, ghostly rhythm. Victor stood in its heart, the silence pressing against his skin like water. The air felt damp, the kind that seeps into bones, filled with the weight of things left unsaid.

Lanterns floated in the distance, each suspended midair like fading memories, dimly glowing, one by one. Each one flickered gently, casting halos of pale gold that pulsed like dying stars. This place wasn't real, and yet it held more truth than any battlefield or council chamber he had ever stood in.

Victor waited. He knew he would come. Soft footsteps. No echo, but just presence. And there he was—walking slowly toward him from the shadows. Alexander looked lost and was searching. He stopped a few feet away, eyes adjusting to the low light. "Where are we?" he asked quietly.

Victor didn't answer right away. He turned to face the first lantern as it bloomed into brightness, revealing the flicker of figures seated around a vast round table carved from black stone. Their faces were obscured by smoke and veils. Yet their presence filled the space with dread.

"The Five Pillars," Victor said at last, his voice deep, steady, and tinged with sorrow. "The architects of the underworld. Each one rules a continent. Together, they shaped the world beneath the surface. A world of shadows, influence, and rot."

Alexander stepped closer. His eyes narrowed, watching the scene flicker within the lantern. "I've heard whispers... but never believed they were real."

"Oh, they're real," Victor said. "The Serpent Gang. Red Tide. Saffron Group. Sahara Nexus. And the Casella family—my so-called family. They've ruled longer than most governments have existed."

He gestured, and the second lantern lit with a hiss. Inside, a boy was thrown into a cold marble chamber. Guards in suits stood at every wall. The boy—alone, no more than ten—stood straight, not crying.

"That was me," Victor said, softly. "Taken in by the Casellas. Groomed in silence. They taught me loyalty. Obedience. Ruthlessness. I learned the art of killing before I learned how to mourn."

Alexander's voice faltered. "They adopted you?"

"They claimed me," Victor corrected. "Used me. When I was older, they sent me across the continents. Africa. South and North America. Asia. I was a ghost—cutting off threats, removing impurities. I wasn't born a killer. I was shaped into one, by the people who called it survival and justice. I believed them for a while."

A third lantern flickered on, this one burning crimson. Victor's jaw clenched. He didn't need to look. He knew what it showed. "They lied. They used me to preserve their rot, not clean it. When I realized what I had become, I tried to fix it. Quietly. I started erasing names. Dismantling smuggling ports. Breaking their financial arteries. I wanted balance. To remove away the diseased parts."

Alexander stared at him. "You tried to bring justice… from the inside?"

Victor nodded slowly. "And they retaliated."

Within the lantern, flames roared. Vehicles burning in an ambush. A boy, not more than seven, lay face-down on the road. A toy car clutched in one hand. A silver bracelet around his wrist. Blood everywhere.

Alexander's breath hitched.

"My son," Victor whispered. "They murdered him using a mercenary squad. Paid by all five. They didn't just want to punish me, they wanted to erase me. End my bloodline. Because I became the impurity."

He turned now, facing Alexander directly. The lanterns flickered around them, casting shadows across Victor's scarred face. "That's when I disappeared. Buried my name.

Burned the past. I tried living like a normal man. Lived quietly. But the wound never closed. I smiled for strangers. But I screamed in silence every night."

Alexander's voice cracked. "Why are you showing me this?"

Victor stepped closer. His voice was softer now, more human. "We are two people, in one body. So it must be sensible that you must know about me. Also, some men chase redemption. I just want silence."

He gestured again. The next lantern showed Alexander, walking alone through ruins, haunted by faces, surrounded by the ghosts of his own uncertainty. "You've walked through the world as if it owed you nothing. And yet, it's placed every burden on your shoulders. Just like me."

Alexander clenched his fists. "I didn't ask for this."

"Neither did I," Victor replied, almost gently. "But we're here. And the war is coming whether we're ready or not. Change isn't a choice anymore. It's the only way forward."

The void began to ripple. The dream began to fall apart like ashes scattering into wind. Victor's voice faded into echo as the lanterns dimmed one by one. "Don't run from what you are, Alexander. When the time comes... don't fight for me. Fight for the balance. Fight for Dante."

Alexander stood in the center of it all. His shirt was wrinkled, knuckles raw, hair falling messily over his eyes.

He looked up at Victor, who stood across from him in silence. "I think I'm going mad."

Alexander's voice was quiet. Shaky. Each word like it was being dragged through his throat. "I—I can't stop thinking. My head—it won't slow down. Even when I smile or even when I joke, it's like there's this clawing in my brain." He held his head with both hands, fingers digging into his scalp. "Like something's behind my head."

Victor said nothing.

"I was supposed to meet Elena for a date. Just one hour. One goddamn normal hour." He laughed bitterly. "I dressed up, practiced my lines, stood in front of the mirror like an idiot."

His hands fell to his sides.

"She didn't show up." He sniffed, swallowing hard. "And I know she's scared. Not of me. But of whatever I've become. The way I talk too fast. The way I stare too long. The way I forget things I just said." He glanced down at his hands, as if they didn't belong to him. "I always dropped the coffee. It spilled everywhere. My hands were shaking too hard to hold the cup sometimes too."

Victor remained still.

"They called me names. Some kids laughed—said I looked like a ghost on meds. I heard one of them whisper, 'Look at him, stuttering like a lunatic.'" Alexander's voice cracked. "I wasn't always like this. I was sharp. Clean. In control. But now, I lose track of what's real and what's not. I wake up in places I don't remember falling asleep in. I talk to myself when no one's there."

He started pacing, movements erratic. "I feel people watching. Even when I'm alone. I feel eyes in the mirror. And when I laugh, it sounds wrong. Like it's someone else laughing *through* me."

Alexander stopped. And for a long second, his voice turned into a whisper. "I'm scared, Victor. I'm scared of what I'm turning into." The silence was deafening. Victor's figure stood in the mist, unmoving, eyes solemn.

Alexander looked at him, eyes pleading. "Say something," he begged. "Please."

But Victor didn't speak. Not a word.

* * * * *

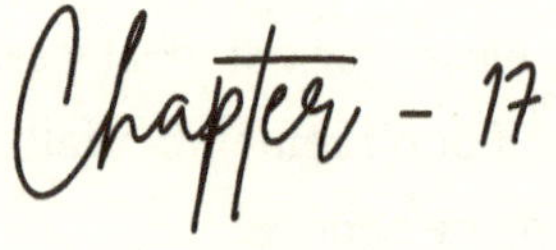

# Chapter - 17

Victor's eyes snapped open, a heavy weight pressing down on his chest as he jolted upright. The faint light of the hotel room filtered through the curtains, casting long shadows across the walls. His mind was still clouded, disoriented from the vivid remnants of his dream. The sense of unease lingered in his veins, like a dark specter that refused to leave.

For a moment, everything felt too quiet—too still.

His gaze flicked toward the empty space beside him. Vanessa wasn't there. His heart skipped a beat, and a cold chill ran down his spine. He quickly glanced around the room, his eyes darting to every corner. She was gone.

A jolt of panic shot through him, and his first instinct was to grab his phone. He checked it quickly, seeing multiple missed calls, dozens of messages, and a slew of notifications from Vanessa.

His chest tightened as the realization set in. Something was wrong. The sinking feeling intensified, and he stood up quickly, his mind racing.

He rushed to the door, his hand gripping the handle tightly as his body tensed, ready for what he feared most. He swung the door open, his footsteps pounding on the hotel floor as he bolted down the hallway. The elevator was out of sight, but he didn't care. He took the stairs two at a time, each step heavy with the weight of impending dread.

Vanessa had been gone for too long. She wouldn't have left without telling him. No, something had happened. Something terrible.

Victor's thoughts raced faster than his feet. His mind flickered back to the last time he saw her. She had gone outside to get some air, but she hadn't returned. He tried to dismiss the nagging feeling that something had gone horribly wrong, but the more he thought about it, the more it gnawed at him. His instincts, honed over years of being in this dangerous world, told him that danger was closer than it ever had been before.

The lobby of the hotel came into view, and he rushed toward the exit, his heart pounding. As he stepped outside, the early morning light washed over him, revealing the empty street. No sign of Vanessa. No sign of anything out of the ordinary.

That's when it hit him. She was gone.

"Vanessa!" he yelled into the empty street, his voice carrying in the stillness. The sound felt wrong, foreign, in the quiet of the morning. His breath came in shallow bursts, and panic began to claw at his chest. "Vanessa!" he called again, his voice breaking with each syllable.

His hands trembled as he dialed her number, but it went straight to voicemail. Another sign of something being terribly wrong. He tried to steady himself, but the feeling of helplessness overwhelmed him. There were no signs of her. No leads. She had vanished.

Victor's chest constricted painfully as his frustration mounted, his thoughts spiraling into a blur of rage and fear. He couldn't lose her, not after everything. Not after everything they had been through. He had already lost too much—too many people, too many connections.

He had sworn he wouldn't lose her too. But now, it seemed as though fate was about to prove him wrong.

Victor's eyes burned with fury as he slammed his phone into his hand. He began pacing back and forth in front of the hotel, his steps rapid and erratic. His mind churned, seeking answers, seeking control of the situation. His body vibrated with the force of the rising storm inside him. He couldn't think straight, his instincts telling him to take action.

"Where the hell are you, Vanessa?" he muttered under his breath, clenching his jaw. His eyes darted around again, scanning the street in desperation.

His breathing grew shallow as the anger bubbled up inside him. The air felt suffocating as his vision blurred with a haze of red. He had to find her. He couldn't wait for the police or anyone else.

Victor's entire body tensed, muscles tight and coiled as he felt the fire within him surge. He had spent years being controlled, being pushed around, trying to bury the man he used to be. But now—now, the rage was back.

He had felt it before. In the dark alleys. In the chaos. That need to destroy. That insatiable thirst for vengeance.

And now, it consumed him.

His hand gripped his phone tightly, and he stared at the empty screen, almost seeing her face in his mind. Vanessa… where the hell were you?

Without thinking, he raised his fist and slammed it against the nearest brick wall with a loud crack. His voice erupted in a primal scream, the force of his anger radiating through the stillness. His breath came in ragged gasps as his chest heaved with frustration.

"Where the hell is she?!" he screamed into the void, his voice echoing off the walls, but it was only met by silence.

His heart raced as his thoughts spiraled further, darker, into a pit he couldn't claw his way out of. He couldn't afford to lose her. Not now.

Victor stood there for a moment, trembling with rage, his mind on the edge of breaking. The silence around him pressed in, suffocating. Vanessa's absence was like an unbearable weight, pulling him deeper into the abyss.

His fists clenched, and he breathed heavily, fighting the urge to lose himself in the rage that surged inside him. But it was no use.

"Dammit," he muttered, his voice low, but full of intent. "I won't let them take you."

Victor didn't wait another second. He stormed back into the hotel, determined to find any trace of her, his steps heavy and purposeful. Every muscle in his body was alert, every instinct focused on finding her. There was no more hesitation. No more waiting.

He would find her. Even if it meant tearing the city apart.

With his jaw set, he muttered to himself as he started the search: "They won't get away with this."

The hunt had just begun.

* * * * *

# Chapter – 18

Victor's heart was still pounding in his chest, the adrenaline coursing through his veins. His mind raced, unable to quiet the storm of thoughts crashing against each other. Every shadow in the street, every passing car felt like an omen. He was spiraling, with his grip on reality beginning to fray, but he couldn't stop. He couldn't slow down.

And then, as if the universe had thrown a wrench into his already shattered focus, his phone rang.

The sound sliced through the tension that had settled over him, freezing him in place. The display flashed an unknown number. A chill ran down his spine, an instinctive feeling that something was wrong. With a shake of his head, Victor reached for his phone, fingers trembling slightly as he answered.

"Hello?" Victor's voice was tight, controlled, though unease coiled just beneath the surface.

The reply came in a low, distorted tone. It wasn't a voice. It was a presence, grating and cold, like metal dragged across stone. It sent a chill through Victor's spine, rooting him in place.

"Vanessa will be gone," the voice said, flat and lifeless. "Just like Dante."

Everything stopped. Victor's grip on the phone tightened as the words sank in. For a second, the world around him seemed to slow, colors bleeding at the edges. His lungs refused to fill, like the air had thickened into something heavy and cruel. And then—Dante. That name hit him like a blow to the ribs.

His voice cracked through the stillness, low and edged with fury. "Grim Reaper. What the hell do you want?"

There was a pause. Then laughter—dry, hollow, the sound of something not quite human. It slithered through the speaker. "You already know who I am, Victor. And you know exactly what I do."

His heart pounded. The stories surged back all at once. The whispers. The warnings. A name spoken in fear, never in daylight. A shadow with no face, no past. A killer that moved like smoke through locked doors and crowded rooms. And that voice. There was no mistaking it now. Victor felt the weight of something ancient pressing down. Something that didn't stop once it started. Something coming.

"I'll never let you do that," Victor spat, his jaw clenched. The rage within him boiled over. Vanessa was everything to him now. He wouldn't allow another person to be taken from him.

The voice didn't reply immediately. There was a long, breathless pause on the other end of the line, followed by a slow, deliberate exhale. "You don't have a choice, Victor," the voice said, the words heavy with finality. "I've been sent. You should have stayed out of the game. But now... it's too late."

Victor's mind was already working, calculating, piecing together what little information he had. His gaze shifted instinctively to the street around him, like the world itself had turned against him. There was no sign of Vanessa. No sign of where she could have gone. And yet...

"Where is she?" Victor demanded, his grip on the phone tightening, his nails digging into his palm. "Tell me where she is, or I swear—"

"You'll be too late," the voice interrupted coldly. "But I'll give you a hint." There was a brief silence, followed by a faint clicking sound, like the Reaper was toying with him, dragging the suspense out to make him squirm. "I'm at the old warehouse in Whitechapel. Come alone, if need to know where she is. I can't guarantee you that she is with me now."

Victor's stomach churned at the words, his body stiffening. Whitechapel. A part of London he knew too well. He didn't hesitate. He didn't need to ask questions. His mind was already set on one thing: getting to her. Before it was too late.

Without a word, he ended the call, his phone slipping from his hand as he immediately moved toward the Aston Martin. The sleek, black Vanquish sat parked in front of the hotel, its curves gleaming in the dim streetlight. Victor didn't waste any time; he threw the door open, sliding into the driver's seat. His hands gripped the wheel tightly as he turned the key, the engine roaring to life.

The sound of the engine, powerful and commanding, was the only thing he could hear in the heavy silence of the night.

His foot slammed down on the gas pedal as he pulled out of the parking lot, tires screeching against the pavement. The city was a blur, buildings passing by like fleeting shadows as he weaved through the streets. His eyes burned with rage, the sharp focus of a man on the edge of something irreversible.

Whitechapel. The name echoed in his mind as he pushed the car faster, feeling the weight of the chase pressing on his chest. The wind whipped through the cracks in the windows, the cold air biting at his face, but Victor didn't feel it. All he could feel was the fire in his veins, the need to protect Vanessa. He would burn down the entire world if it meant saving her.

The streets became darker the closer he got to Whitechapel, the familiar areas of London now unfamiliar, cold, and oppressive. The narrow alleyways, the distant sounds of the city fading into eerie silence. It felt like the calm before a storm. Victor's grip on the wheel tightened as he approached the outskirts of the old industrial district, where the warehouses stood like dark monoliths, abandoned and forgotten.

His mind flashed back to the countless times he had navigated these streets, when he was part of something bigger. When he was part of the chaos. And now, he was back—back in the heart of it all. The grim reaper waiting for him, and Vanessa was caught in the web of it all.

Victor pulled up to a warehouse at the edge of Whitechapel, its rusted metal doors hanging half open, like the entrance to a tomb. The dim glow of a lone streetlamp cast an eerie light on the surroundings, illuminating the shadows that seemed to stretch endlessly.

He parked the Aston Martin and stepped out, his boots clicking against the pavement as he made his way toward the warehouse. Every step was measured, each one bringing him closer to the one person who could ruin everything.

But he wasn't going to let that happen. As he reached the entrance, he hesitated for a split second. The air felt thick, charged with tension. His senses were on high alert. He could feel the weight of the past pressing down on him, the ghosts of those he had lost lingering in the corners of his mind.

He squared his shoulders and pushed the heavy door open. The sound of the creaking hinges echoed through the warehouse, reverberating in the silence. Inside, the shadows seemed to swallow him whole, the faintest flicker of light barely cutting through the darkness.

And then, from the shadows, he heard a voice. A low, gravelly laugh. "You're here," the voice crooned. "Just like I knew you would be."

Victor stepped further into the darkness, his eyes scanning for movement. The warehouse felt like a trap. A spider's web, closing in around him. But he wasn't afraid. Not yet. "You should've stayed out of this," the voice continued, its tone mocking. "You think you can save her? You think you can stop me?"

Victor's fists clenched at his sides as he moved deeper into the warehouse. "Where is she?" he demanded again, his voice low, dangerous. "Tell me, or I swear—"

"Or what?" The voice sneered. "You'll kill me? You'll stop me? You're too late, Victor. It's already over."

The voice fell silent, and Victor's heart stopped. The ominous feeling that had settled in his chest now grew unbearable. Something was wrong. Vanessa wasn't here.

The Grim Reaper had already won.

* * * * *

# Chapter – 19

The warehouse loomed in the distance, like a forgotten relic in Whitechapel. Rust clung to its metal walls, and the rain was relentless, tapping against the corrugated roof like the ghost of distant footsteps. The floorboards creaked beneath the weight of old memories, broken crates scattered like forgotten skeletons. The only light was a flickering bulb above, casting faint shadows that danced and writhed as though alive.

Victor pushed open the crooked door with a slow, deliberate motion. His coat was soaked, the chill of the night biting through the fabric. His fists were clenched, and his eyes had that faraway look, just like someone who had been through too many storms and lost count of how many he'd survived. Still, there was something sharp in his gaze. Something that told you he was not finished yet.

In the center of the dim space stood the Grim Reaper. Cloaked in black, face hidden beneath a bone-carved mask that seemed to glow faintly in the low light, he stood as still as death itself.

Victor stepped forward, the door creaking behind him, and closed it quietly. He didn't need to say much— his presence spoke louder than any words could. His voice, however, was cold and direct as he cut through the silence.

"You called me here," Victor said, his tone flat but heavy with unspoken tension. "Speak."

The Reaper tilted his head, slow and calculating. There was no warmth in his voice, only the sound of inevitability. "Dante is gone, isn't he?"

Victor's jaw tightened. He didn't answer right away, just stood there, frozen for a moment. Then, his words came through gritted teeth. "Say that again."

The Reaper's voice was almost bored now, as if it was a trivial thing. "Dante, the one I had killed. Without mercy and without honor. The last breath he drew was under my guns."

Victor's eyes flashed with rage. His fingers twitched. The words "Dante" and "death" did not sit well in his chest.

Without thinking, without warning, Victor lunged. His first connected with the Reaper's mask, the sound of impact cracking through the quiet warehouse. The Reaper staggered, but only for a moment.

Victor didn't stop. He followed with a vicious right hook to the ribs and then shoved the masked figure back into a stack of crates. He was a man pushed beyond reason, beyond control. "You wear his death like a medal!" Victor roared, the words more like a wound than a yell. "You stood by while he was killed!"

The Reaper's laugh was low and guttural, like the sound of bones scraping together. He surged forward, his speed unmatched as he caught Victor's next punch mid-air, twisting his arm with an expert motion. A sharp knee to Victor's stomach left him gasping for air, but he refused to fall.

Victor headbutted him with all his remaining strength, cracking the mask slightly at the corner. Blood dripped from his lip, mixing with the sweat on his face, but did not reveal the man behind the mask.

"I'm not your pawn," Victor growled, his voice raw with emotion. "I buried my son. I won't burn this world for anyone else."

The Reaper pushed him back, breathing hard. There was something unsettling about how calm he remained. Something predatory. He spoke with a voice that carried no sympathy—only cold calculation. "You're still emotional," the Reaper hissed. "You think this is about loyalty or vengeance. But this..." His voice dropped, becoming low and ominous. "This is about balance."

Victor wiped blood from his lip, glaring at the Reaper, unwilling to back down. "Don't lecture me about balance while you trade in bodies. I know what balance is about."

The Reaper exhaled, an almost imperceptible sigh, and took a step closer. "You're too blinded by your emotions. This isn't about what you think Victor. This is about the Casella empire. It needs these small two syndicates eliminated."

Victor's gaze darkened. "What syndicates?"

The Reaper didn't answer immediately. Instead, he reached into his coat, producing a bloodstained folder. It hit the crate with a thud. He didn't need to explain. The photo, the names, the addresses were all were self-explanatory.

"There are two syndicates causing problems for the Casella empire," the Reaper said, his tone now clipped. "One in London. One in Monaco. Both are small, but disruptive. If they aren't eliminated, the empire will fall apart."

Victor opened the folder, scanning the contents. Two names stood out. Rafiq Al-Mir, the London cell leader, and Marcus Volanti, the Monaco trafficker.

"The Casella empire," Victor muttered, as his fingers gripped the folder tightly. "And Vanessa?"

The Reaper's mask seemed to almost smile, though it was impossible to tell beneath the bone-carved surface. "Vanessa is in the hands of Giovanni and Leonardo Casella," he replied. "They've got her locked up in an estate in their villa in Rome. Not dead yet. But she's a bargaining chip."

Victor's gaze hardened. "Bargaining chip?"

The Reaper's voice dropped to a whisper. "For you to cooperate. For you to do what's necessary to keep things in order. You eliminate the syndicates, and then you'll have your chance to make contact. You'll have your chance to save her."

Victor's hands shook, but not from fear. From rage. From the recognition that he was once again being forced to make choices that were beyond his control.

"Why don't you do it?" Victor snapped, his voice sharp. "You're good at killing, blackmailing, hiding in the shadows."

The Reaper shrugged. "I'm a busy man. Contract killings all over the world. Seoul, Madrid, Bucharest... I've got my hands full." He leaned closer, his voice soft but commanding. "But you? You're the one who's here, and you're the one who can do this. These tasks will give you leverage. You just need to finish them."

Victor closed the folder, his eyes narrowing. "And if I don't?"

The Reaper's mask seemed to shift slightly, as if the smile deepened, though it was only a trick of the light. "If you don't, Vanessa dies. Slowly."

Victor's breath caught in his chest, and for a moment, he couldn't speak. The weight of the ultimatum pressed down on him like a heavy stone.

The Reaper turned, disappearing into the mist, his voice lingering. "I'll be waiting. But don't take too long."

Victor stood in silence, staring at the empty space where the Reaper had been. His hands trembled, not from fear, but from the weight of everything that had been thrown at him. His chest ached, the pain of losing Dante and the weight of his son's death still fresh, gnawing at him.

"I'll be waiting," he whispered to the shadows.

His gaze fell to the folder. He opened it again and saw the photos of Rafiq Al-Mir and Marcus Volanti, two men who were as good as dead.

But then, there was something else. Another page in the folder. Something he hadn't noticed before. A question.

"The Library of Secrets?" Victor muttered under his breath. He wasn't sure why it mattered, but it did. The Reaper had asked. The Casella empire had asked.

And somewhere deep inside him, Victor knew that the key to the Library of Secrets was still hidden. Somewhere hidden in a secret place that Victor had hoped that would not be shown to anyone else. He hid that years ago, unsure of the key's fate now.

Suddenly, Alexander's voice broke through his mind like a whisper in a storm. "In my language, that's a lot to ask, don't you think, mate?"

Victor's lips twisted into a dry smile, but it didn't reach his eyes. He looked up at the rain-slicked streets outside and then back at the photos. "This is what I do. Kill people for a better world in my sense."

*　*　*　*　*

# Chapter - 20

Victor stood alone on the edge of a derelict rooftop, one hand buried deep in his coat pocket, the other gripping an old burner phone. Fog curled at his boots like ghosts.

He dialed. A few rings. Then Victor spoke up. "Cyrus."

There was a pause on the other end. Then a chuckle. "Well. I thought you were dead, Victor."

Victor didn't laugh. "I nearly was."

Another pause. A breath. Then, calmly: "I heard about Dante."

Victor said nothing. His silence was heavy enough to answer.

Cyrus Montclair had once been a storm in military uniform. A prodigy of the French Foreign Legion, he served in clandestine wars across Africa and Eastern Europe, gaining a reputation not only for precision kills but for an unnerving ability to predict chaos before it happened. When he left the Legion, he didn't retire—he adapted.

A man of tailored suits and silver pistols, Cyrus became an arms dealer, a fixer, and a friend to the shadows. But only to a few.

Victor had been one of them.

"I need you in Manchester," Victor said.

"Business?" Cyrus asked, his tone tightening.

"Worse," Victor replied. "Personal."

"You're bringing me back into the fire?"

Victor looked out across the rainy skyline. "You still keep that bag?"

"The one labeled 'In Case of the End of the World'?" Cyrus asked. "Always."

"I want that bag," Victor said. "Tomorrow night. The Marisela Hotel, Manchester. Quiet entrance. Nine o'clock. Bring what you can carry. Nothing less."

Cyrus exhaled, slowly. "Are we going for the reaper again, Harrington?"

Victor's voice dropped. "Not yet. But soon."

"Understood. Remember this Victor. When you start killing gods, you need the devil on your side."

Victor closed the phone and pocketed it. No goodbyes were needed.

Thunder rolled in the distance, low and threatening. He pulled his coat tighter, already walking toward the stairwell down from the roof. In his coat was the folder. And in the folder—names. Faces. Rafiq Al-Mir. Marcus Volanti.

Before long, blood would be in the streets again.

And Victor would be the one holding the knife.

* * * *

# Chapter - 21

The streets of Whitechapel were slick with rain, glistening like obsidian under the early morning light. Victor stood by the Aston Martin, the engine humming low. He looked up at the grey sky once more, then stepped into the driver's seat and closed the door.

The wipers moved in rhythm, brushing away the tears of the city. The road ahead was quiet—London had not yet stirred from its slumber. Victor drove with no music, no radio, just the murmur of rain against metal and the slow, aching beat of his thoughts.

An hour later, he was at the Highgate cemetery.

It stretched before him in silence—rows of old stones jutting from the damp earth like memories half-forgotten. Trees stood like sentinels, still and shrouded in fog. Victor walked with his hands in his coat, shoes crunching wet gravel. He knew the way.

Dante's grave was modest. A black stone, polished smooth, with his name etched in quiet dignity. No grand epitaph. Just the dates. And the loss.

Victor stood still for a moment. He had no words. He never did when he was here. There was too much to say and too little meaning left in language. "I still hear your voice sometimes," he murmured, eyes fixed on the stone. "Not in the wind. Not in dreams. Just... inside. Like an echo that refuses to leave."

He crouched, brushing some leaves from the base of the grave. The silence pressed in like a hand on his chest. "Am I doing the right thing?" he asked. "Or just pretending I know what right even is?"

From a few rows away, he heard a soft voice. "She was buried last spring."

Victor turned. An older man in his late sixties, stood over a grave, holding a faded umbrella. His suit was too formal for the mud, his tie crooked like he hadn't noticed.

"I'm sorry?" Victor asked gently.

"My wife," the man said, nodding to the grave. "Fifty years together. Cancer took her in six months."

Victor lowered his gaze. "I'm sorry for your loss."

The man smiled faintly. "I've stopped saying 'thank you' to that. It doesn't really make a difference, does it?"

Victor didn't reply.

"She used to tell me that time heals everything," the man went on, voice a bit rougher now. "But what she didn't say was that the healing doesn't mean it stops hurting. It just means you get used to breathing with a hole in your chest."

Victor looked back at Dante's grave.

"She was the better part of me," the man said. "And without her, I feel like I've been left behind in a world that no longer knows my name."

Victor finally spoke. "I lost my son."

The man looked at him, sympathy blooming in his eyes. "Then we're both just strangers in a world that kept moving without us."

Victor nodded slowly. "I don't know if I'm angrier that he's gone... or that I'm still here."

The man placed a hand on his own chest. "That's the curse of the living, isn't it? To carry what the dead no longer can."

A long silence passed between them. The rain had softened now, more of a mist. The fog hung still.

Victor turned to go.

"Take care of yourself," the man said, gently. "Even broken spirits still have moments of truth."

Victor managed the faintest smile. "You too."

As he walked back toward the car, he felt the weight settle deeper in his spine. He slid behind the wheel, resting his hands on the steering column. His reflection stared back at him from the rearview mirror. He was tired, hollow, haunted.

He started the engine. The Aston Martin roared softly to life.

* * * *

# Chapter - 22

The Aston Martin's engine purred beneath the cold drizzle of dusk, waiting like a beast beneath Victor's steady hands. He slid into the driver's seat of the car, its leather still damp from the last night's storm. The folder lay on the passenger seat—slightly open—exposing a grainy photograph of a man in a leather jacket, Rafiq Al-Mir, grinning like he owned the night.

Victor sat in silence, staring through the fogged windshield at the blurred outline of Whitechapel behind him. Then he sighed, long and heavy.

"Your turn." Victor muttered under his breath. The shift was subtle. Like a shadow exhaling.

Alexander blinked, now behind the wheel.

He looked down at the folder and reached over, flipping through its pages with nervous fingers. "Rafiq Al-Mir," he murmured. "Manchester. Barlow Estates. Mugging people. Trafficking." His voice trailed as he read the part about foreigners being targeted, beaten. Guns. Violence. No arrests. No hope.

Alexander's grip tightened on the edge of the page. "We should call the police."

"Absolutely not."

Victor's voice echoed sharp and cold in his mind.

Alexander narrowed his eyes. "Why not?"

"You think the police are going to walk into a MI6-linked syndicate and not trace it back to us? Vanessa's a ghost. A missing MI6 agent. And we're being watched."

"But they're criminals!" Alexander snapped, pulling out his phone. "Let the law deal with it!"

He started dialing. 9-9-9, and froze. Alexander could not move his hand.

It wouldn't move. "What...?" He looked at his hand, still hovering over the screen, fingers stiff, locked like stone.

"You—" he breathed. "You're controlling me."

"I'm stopping you from destroying everything." Victor's tone was calm, too calm. "You want to play innocent, but you live in a world where innocence gets buried six feet under."

Alexander gritted his teeth, straining his hand. It refused to obey. "I'm not like you," he hissed. "I still believe there's right and wrong."

"And that belief will get her killed."

Alexander fell back into the seat, breathing heavily, his mind storming with conflict. "You think this is the only way."

"It is. These syndicates won't stop because you ask nicely. We need to burn them out. Fast. Quiet. Clean."

"But there has to be—there has to be some other option," Alexander said quietly.

"There isn't. You want to be the man who saves Vanessa? Then accept the world you're in. Not the one you wish existed."

For a long moment, Alexander just stared out at the road ahead. The rain had softened into a mist, and the lights of Manchester glowed faintly in the distance. He closed the folder, tucked it under his arm, and placed both hands on the wheel.

Then he whispered, with something broken in his voice, "Alright. Let's see how dirty my hands need to get."

He accelerated into drive. The Aston Martin roared forward, headlights cutting through fog and steel. As the city swallowed them, Victor stayed silent.

But Alexander, biting his lip, forced a shaky laugh.

"This is a lot to ask, mate," he muttered in his best deadpan British accent. "Kill two gangs, find Vanessa, and unlock a mythical library of secrets? What's next? Tea with the devil?"

Victor didn't reply.

The only answer was the sound of the engine, carrying them faster into the heart of Manchester, and into whatever fire waited there.

* * * *

# Chapter - 23

Manchester pulsed with life. The city streets were wet but alive, full of motion, music, and a thousand conversations happening all at once. Neon lights danced off puddles on the ground, buses rumbled past packed cafes, and the aroma of fresh kebabs, cigarettes, and warm bread filled the air. It was a Friday evening, and the streets buzzed with a mix of locals, tourists, and restless souls chasing distraction.

The Aston Martin turned off a main street and slipped quietly through the back lanes toward the quieter part of town. The engine purred like a restrained animal beneath the rain-slicked hood. Alexander was still. His fingers drummed softly against the steering wheel, eyes distant. The streetlamps cast gold and silver ribbons through the window as they passed.

When they finally pulled into the curb across from The Marisela Hotel, it looked like a jewel tucked between forgotten buildings. Its art-deco architecture stood proud, which was subtle but elegant, with warm amber lights glowing from inside.

Jazz music could be heard faintly through the glass doors. Bellhops helped guests in tailored coats, laughter spilled from a group leaving for dinner, and taxis honked in the distance. It was the kind of place where time moved slower. Safer.

Alexander exhaled shakily, opened the door, and stepped out.

The air was damp but cool, filled with the buzz of city life. He pulled up his coat collar and locked the car with a click. Across the street, a group of men leaned against a brick wall outside a betting shop. Hoodies up. Smoke curling from their lips. They looked up when he passed. One of them smirked.

Alexander felt it. A gaze that lingered a second too long. He quickened his pace, eyes forward. He was almost at the hotel entrance. Just a few more steps.

The footsteps followed. A voice called out, casual but sharp. "Oi mate! Lost?"

Alexander turned his head slightly. Five men. All local. All watching him like wolves circling a meal. He tried to keep walking.

"Hold up," another said, stepping in front of him. "You deaf or just rude?"

Alexander stopped. "I don't want trouble."

"Oh, good. Neither do we," the tall one grinned, stepping closer. "But we still found you. Which means Rafiq wants to see you."

One of them pulled a knife. Just a flash of metal, not raised, but it was with him. Another flicked a lighter, letting the flame dance before blowing it out with a grin. The gang surrounded him in a casual, practiced formation, just out of reach of the hotel cameras, just deep enough in shadow.

"I'm just checking in," Alexander muttered.

The leader gave a theatrical shrug. "Checking in? Mate, you're checking *out*."

The first punch came hard, straight to his stomach. Air shot from Alexander's lungs. He doubled over. Then another hit, this time to the face. Someone grabbed his jacket and slammed him against the wall. His knees buckled. His head rang.

Around them, the street was still alive. People walked past, some glanced, most didn't. A few slowed, but no one stepped in. This was Rafiq's block. Everyone knew it. Law had no say here.

"This him?" one of the gang member muttered, kicking Alexander's leg.

"Yeah. This is the one."

A boot drove into his side. The taste of blood hit his tongue. His vision blurred. Another kick. More laughter. He tried to crawl, but a hand pinned him to the wet ground.

And then there was silence. There was no pain, no sound, but just a static hum. Alexander blacked out. When

Alexander blinked again, he was alone. The gang was stumbling back. One man was on the ground, groaning.

Alexander had a knife in his hand. Blood along the edge. Not his blood. Alexander gasped and dropped it with a clatter.

"No, no—what—" he stammered. "I didn't—" He looked around. The others backed off, not afraid of him—but of what just took over. Of someone else.

Victor's voice echoed faintly in his head. "There you go. Job done."

Alexander turned and ran—limping, breath short.

The Marisela Hotel glowed just ahead, golden and warm. The doorman stepped aside as if expecting him. He didn't say a word. He stumbled into the elevator, hands trembling. As the doors closed, he caught his reflection in the mirrored wall.

He leaned against the elevator wall, eyes wide. "Cyrus booked this room for us," he whispered to himself. "Just a quiet check-in."

But nothing was quiet anymore.

* * * * *

# Chapter - 24

The door closed with a soft click behind Alexander.

It was dimly lit, with rich colored curtains drawn against the Manchester skyline, warm light spilling from a lamp over a low coffee table. The room smelled faintly of cologne and old wood. A vintage armchair sat across from a king-size bed, and a fireplace screen displayed a flickering simulation of embers.

Alexander stood still, body sore, jaw bruised, and blood drying on his coat. He looked at his shaking hands, at the splatter on his sleeve. He closed his eyes.

And when they opened again, He was Victor Harrington once more. The stillness returned. The air itself seemed to settle around him. The erratic tremors ceased, his shoulders straightened, and something colder took its place.

Victor walked calmly to the sink, washed the blood from his hands, then opened the minibar and poured himself a glass of water. His reflection in the mirror was quiet. Ready.

A knock came. Three soft taps.

Victor opened the door without hesitation.

Cyrus stepped inside the room. His hair was swept back, face lined with wear but still striking. He had the gait of a man who had seen too much, but forgot nothing. In his right hand, he carried a worn leather duffel bag, heavier than it looked.

"Well," Cyrus smirked, closing the door behind him, "you didn't waste any time. Heard there was a bit of theatre downstairs. Quite the show."

Victor didn't smile. "I don't recall applauding."

Cyrus chuckled under his breath. "Still sharp. That's good. You'll need that."

He dropped the duffel onto the bed and unzipped it. Inside, nestled in foam cutouts, were firearms, all sleek and deadly. A custom matte-black pistol. A silenced SMG. Many other firearms were inside the duffel bag. A sawed-off shotgun with a carbon grip. Extra magazines. Ammunition in labeled packs. Grenades, smoke bombs. There were all tools for ghosts, not soldiers.

Next to it, folded with care, was a new outfit—casual, but fully reinforced with military-grade bulletproof layering. Black. Lightweight. Stylish. Built for mobility and survival.

Victor looked at it all in silence.

"Rome," Cyrus said, watching him, "won't be easy. You know that. Every step between here and there will test your will. People will try to slow you down. Stop you. Break you."

Victor's eyes remained on the weapons. "Let them try."

Cyrus's voice softened. "And when you get to her… Vanessa. What then?"

Victor looked up. Silence lingered. "I haven't thought that far," he replied. His voice low, restrained.

Cyrus nodded slowly. "I'm sorry about Dante. Truly. He was a good one."

Victor blinked. "You're two years late."

A pause. Then Cyrus nodded again. "Fair. But still, my condolences."

Victor gave a slight nod, then zipped the bag partially, checking the weight.

Cyrus stepped toward the door. "If you need anything, call me. I may not be in the field anymore, but my reach still covers the darker corners."

Victor stopped him just before he left. "The Inferno mercenaries. Are they still under your command?"

Cyrus raised an eyebrow. "Still loyal. Still waiting. Say the word."

Victor's mouth curved, barely. "Good."

As Cyrus reached for the door handle, Victor added, "Thank you. For the bag."

Cyrus looked back, his voice laced with an old kind of affection. "That's not a bag, Vic. That's a portable apocalypse." And with that, he disappeared into the hallway.

Victor stood alone in the hotel room, looking down at the weapons, the gear, the armor.

* * * * *

#  Chapter - 25

The hum of the city beyond the hotel windows was muffled, as if the walls themselves knew what was coming.

Victor stood in the center of the room, steam rising around him. The shower had been long, almost too long, but necessary. Hot water had poured over his shoulders, calming the ache of bruised ribs, rinsing off blood and dust from the alley.

He stood still for a moment after it ended, staring at himself in the fogged mirror. His body carried the quiet map of violence. Faint scars across ribs, wrists, and a pale burn above the left collarbone. He ran a hand through his wet hair. The reflection blinked and what blinked back was no longer a man grieving.

It was him, on a mission. He stepped out of the bathroom with a towel around his waist. Then, slowly, deliberately, he began to suit up.

First came the base layer, which was a stretch-weave undersuit lined with ballistic fiber, hugging his frame like a second skin. Over that, a dark combat shirt, Kevlar-threaded and flame resistant. His pants were armored, sleek, and flexible, which was enough to run, dive, and bleed in.

Then the vest. Tight, weighted, customized to his shape. Magazine pouches sat snug on the chest, just under the heart. His signature shoulder holster locked into place—left for the silenced pistol, right for the blade.

He opened the duffel and laid out the weapons on the bed. He took two pistols which were fully loaded, a short curved knife and one smoke grenade.

His boots laced tightly. Lightweight. Reinforced soles. Good for silent movement. Victor zipped the duffel shut, stood tall, checked the chamber of both pistols, and exhaled.

Then, he stepped into the hallway of the hotel, black coat swirling as he moved like a shadow carved out of purpose.

* * * *

Elsewhere in Manchester, Rafiq's Turf was in his Estate, Eastside Industrial Block.

Inside a warehouse masked as a repair garage, a small-time lookout watched a grainy CCTV monitor. His phone buzzed.

"Boss," the thug muttered into the phone, chewing gum, "he's moving. Just left the hotel."

Silence on the other end. Then a voice—low and amused.

"Finally."

The lookout wiped his mouth, nervous. "Should I—?"

"Don't move. Just watch."

The line cut.

Downstairs, beneath the garage, twenty men were already gathering. Some sharpening blades. Others checking rifles. Their eyes were hard, which were military-hardened, ex-mercs now loyal to Rafiq's pocket.

At the center, a tall figure in a leather coat stood silently, holstering twin gold-plated pistols., was Rafiq's most brutal lieutenant. He cracked his neck. "Victor Harrington," he said with a crooked smile. "Looks like he wants to dance."

The men around him laughed in dark, eager sounds.

"Gear up," the lieutenant ordered, voice low. "No survivors. And tell Rafiq that his guest is on the way."

* * * * *

# Chapter - 26

The Aston Martin slid to a slow, graceful stop on the gravel path in front of the Azim Estate, its engine purring like a restrained beast. The air in Manchester was cool, crisp, humming with faint city noise in the far distance. The sun hung high, watching silently.

Victor Harrington stepped out of the car and adjusted his collar. He exhaled and then walked. Ahead, lit by amber floodlights and cigarette tips, stood twenty men, which were Rafiq's foot soldiers. They leaned on bikes, trucks, crates. Some laughed. Some didn't bother looking up. But they all knew who he was.

And behind them, like a king watching over pawns, stood Rafiq Al-Rahman, dressed in a sharp maroon blazer and loafers, gold chain resting on his chest, chewing a toothpick with arrogance.

"Victor Harrington," Rafiq called with theatrical delight. "Twenty million euros on your head. You're a walking myth, mate." Victor didn't respond. His eyes scanned the gang, calculating, memorizing their positions, weapons, spacing.

Rafiq chuckled. "Come on, you're not even going to ask me to surrender?"

Victor's voice was cold. "No."

The first man to die never saw it coming. A lean thug with a mohawk stepped forward, cocky, raising a pistol lazily. Victor's body blurred forward in a burst. He grabbed the man's wrist mid-draw, twisted until the bone cracked. The scream didn't even leave the man's throat before Victor jammed his pistol under his chin and pulled the trigger.

The shot echoed like thunder. The body dropped, twitching.

Victor blinked, watching the blood pool beneath the man's face. And for the first time in years, he smiled.

There was a rush, a ripple through his spine. A high he'd forgotten. Not fear. Not vengeance.

Joy.

"God, I missed this," he murmured, almost surprised at himself.

A shot pierced the air. Another thug dropped like a sack of bricks, a clean headshot through the eye. The place exploded into chaos.

Victor moved like a storm, like always graceful, lethal and precise.

He spun left, fired two shots. One hit a man's kneecap; the other hit his forehead before he even had time to scream. The next thug lunged with a machete—Victor ducked, grabbed his wrist, twisted, and jammed his pistol under the man's chin—bang. Blood splattered the concrete.

Gunfire echoed. Victor sprinted low, slid behind a metal drum, reloaded in half a second, popped up and aimed and shot at two more heads.

A brute with a crowbar charged. Victor holstered his weapon mid-run, drew his knife, sidestepped, slashed across the man's chest, and stabbed him in the thigh. The man howled. Victor twisted the blade, then kicked him down and stomped his skull against the pavement.

Five down.

A shotgun blast grazed his shoulder. Victor flinched, rolled behind a column, tossed a flashbang grenade.

Screams and disorientation occurred soon.

Victor burst out, firing his gun in controlled bursts. Three men went down before they even raised their weapons—one with a bullet through the temple, another through the throat, the third through the eye socket. He spun, disarmed a fourth with a swift elbow strike, kicked his gun away, and shot him through the heart mid-fall.

Ten down.

Two came from behind—Victor ducked, caught one in a judo throw, shot the other in the leg, and crushed the first attacker's neck between his knees, then calmly turned and shot the second in the mouth.

A fistfight broke out with three charging thugs. Victor went hand-to-hand, dodging a punch, elbowing a jaw, grabbing one man's head and slamming it into the hood of a nearby car. The next man pulled a knife—Victor caught the wrist, redirected the blade, and forced it into the thug's chest. He shoved the dying man into the last one and fired through both of them.

Seventeen down.

The last three tried to run. Victor threw a knife into the back of one. The second turned—only to catch a bullet between the ribs. The third? Victor took his time—walked over, kicked his legs out, and shot him cleanly through the heart as he screamed.

The courtyard went silent.

Smoke floated. The scent of blood and cordite lingered. Bodies lay sprawled in pools of red. Casings sparkled like metal confetti.

Victor stood in the middle, eyes calm, guns still smoking. Breathing slow. Unshaken.

Only Rafiq remained. His smirk had vanished. His fingers twitched as if debating a retreat. But it was too late for that.

"You... you're a monster," Rafiq whispered.

Victor holstered one pistol. The other stayed raised. "You hired twenty men," Victor said softly. "You should've brought fifty."

Victor stood tall, gun raised, staring coldly into Rafiq's terrified eyes. The man who had once spoken with swagger now trembled, the blood of twenty loyal men soaking the ground around him. Victor's finger hovered on the trigger—steady, ready.

But inside him, something shifted. A voice. Alexander. "Victor, wait."

Victor's jaw clenched.

"Listen to me. Killing him... it's easy. You've done worse. But think about this. This man knows every alley in Manchester's underworld. Every dealer, every smuggler, every contact here. What if we keep him? Let him live not for mercy, but strategy. Keep him scared. Keep him useful."

Victor didn't speak. His hand twitched once.

"Peace is a weapon too," Alexander urged from within. "We don't have time for every war. You need to get to Rome. Saving Vanessa will make you remember why we're doing this."

Victor exhaled slowly. Then he lowered the gun.

Rafiq collapsed to his knees, breath caught in his throat, staring up in disbelief at the man who had just slaughtered an army and spared him.

Victor leaned in coldly, voice low and sharp: "You're alive because I let you be. From now on, you work for me. Cross me once and your death won't be this quick."

Rafiq only nodded, too shaken to speak.

Victor turned away, his coat swaying behind him, leaving blood and silence in his wake.

*  *  *  *  *

# Chapter - 27

Victor drove with precision—never reckless, never hesitant. The speedometer climbed steadily as the streets emptied. A man on a mission.

His phone lit up on the dashboard. He tapped the screen and spoke calmly. The line rang once.

"Victor," Cyrus answered quickly. "What's going on?"

"I need a jet," Victor said. "Manchester Airport. Destination to Paris. Quiet and immediate."

A pause. Then the faint sound of Cyrus typing. "Hangar 12. G650. Pilot's ready," Cyrus confirmed, but there was tension in his voice. "You're going to him, aren't you?"

"Yes."

"You know Silvio Arcuri won't welcome you with champagne."

Victor exhaled, turning onto the expressway. "I'm not expecting champagne."

Cyrus's voice lowered, cautious now. "Victor, this isn't a simple meeting. You put his son, Matteo to death. Arcuri remembers. He always does. He might hold that grudge."

"I know."

"Then why go?" Cyrus asked, almost pleading. "There are other ways."

"There aren't," Victor replied firmly. "This is the last thread left. The Casella Empire's hands are tightening again, I need to dismantle that empire and get Vanessa soon. La Rosa Nera is the only syndicate that ever stood against them without fear. If there's any chance to stop what's coming, it starts with Silvio."

Cyrus sighed heavily on the other end. "Just be careful. You're walking into a conversation that could end with a bullet."

"I'm counting on the conversation to come first."

Minutes later, Victor pulled into Manchester Airport, the engine sound of the Aston Martin fading as he approached the private terminal. The sky above was clear, dotted with stars, the air sharp and cool.

Waiting near Hangar 12 stood Cyrus, dressed in a dark coat, arms folded, eyes locked on the approaching car. Victor pulled up smoothly, stopped, and stepped out without a word. The jet behind Cyrus was already powered, its lights glowing softly, casting long shadows on the tarmac.

"Right on time," Cyrus said, catching the car keys Victor tossed him.

"She's yours until I get back," Victor said.

"You better come back," Cyrus muttered, watching Victor closely. "Silvio's not the kind of man who forgets. He might offer a seat, a drink, and a smile. But trust me, he's got Matteo's face burned into his mind."

"I'm not going there as a Casella," Victor said, adjusting the collar of his coat. "I'm going as something else. And if Silvio's half the strategist I believe he is, he'll know this is an opportunity... not a trap."

"And if he doesn't?"

Victor paused, then smirked faintly. "Then I'm glad you've got good taste in suits. Send something nice to the funeral."

Cyrus didn't smile.

Victor climbed the steps to the Gulfstream G650, the engines now humming. As the door closed behind him, the night outside seemed to stretch on in silence.

* * * * *

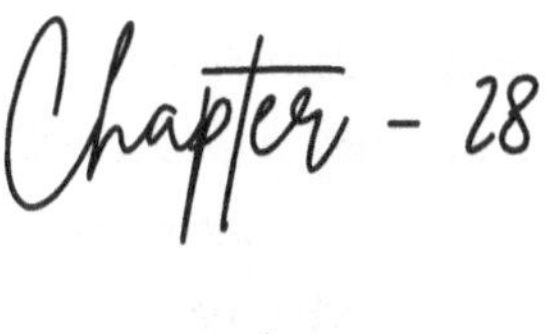

# Chapter - 28

The night in Paris was still, almost aristocratic in its quiet. From the balcony of his private villa in Montmorency, overlooking the distant glow of the city, Don Silvio Arcuri stood in his tailored midnight suit, a glass of aged Brunello di Montalcino in hand. He didn't smile often these days—there were few things left that surprised him.

But this evening, he was intrigued.

A soft knock came at the door of his study. Then it opened without waiting. Gianni, his most trusted man, stepped inside. His eyes were sharp. Alert. "Don Arcuri," he said carefully. "He's coming."

Silvio didn't need to ask who. There have been reports of Victor's movements in London. He turned slowly from the balcony, placing his wine glass down on the marble sill.

"Victor Harrington," he said with quiet weight. "So, he finally grows into his own legend."

Gianni nodded. "Just landed in Paris. The pilot confirmed. Gulfstream G650. Unregistered flight path. No Casella insignia. Maybe he is on his own."

Silvio walked into his study, the floor beneath him silent, the rugs imported from Florence cushioning his steps. He stopped beside the fire, where a small silver frame sat. Inside it was a photograph of Matteo, his only son. A younger version of the boy, before what had happened in Rome.

He picked up the frame and stared at it for a moment. The light from the flames flickered across his face, dancing shadows where rage and memory mingled.

"Victor and I know what he did to my Matteo," Silvio said, his voice cool and composed. "The boy was left bleeding in his own home like some stray dog. His pride was ripped out."

Gianni kept his voice low. "Would you like him turned away?"

"No."

Silvio placed the frame down gently. "If he comes now, after all these years, knowing what blood lies between us— he comes with purpose. And I want to hear it."

He walked back toward the window and motioned subtly. "Double the guards on the north wall. Position snipers on the tower and eastern terrace. No one gets near the house without my word."

Gianni nodded. "And the villa itself?" he asked.

"Triple security inside. Discreet but present. I want my men at every hallway turn, armed but silent. No one raises a hand unless I say so."

Silvio turned back toward him. "Send a car. The black Porsche, not the armored one. We'll give him respect... not fear."

Gianni raised a brow. "And if he brought more than words?"

Silvio's gaze hardened. "Then he'll die where Matteo should have."

There was a long pause.

"Prepare for a dinner," Silvio added after a moment. "I want him to feel comfort. Men like Victor speak more freely when they think they're not in danger."

"And if he's not the same man you once knew?"

"Then I'll know," Silvio whispered.

Gianni bowed slightly and left the room, his boots echoing faintly down the marble hallway.

Silvio turned back toward the night, watching the lights of the city that once belonged to kings.

So, Victor Harrington was coming. Not as a Casella, not as an enemy, But as something else.

The Don took another sip of his wine, the bitterness curling on his tongue like memory. "Welcome to my garden, Victor," he murmured. "Let's see if your thorns are still sharp."

* * * * *

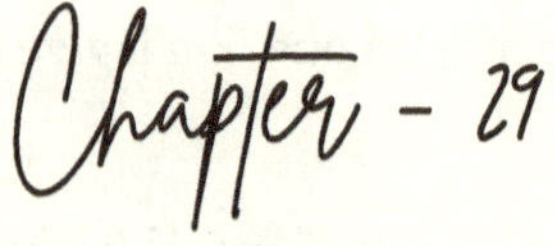



The Gulfstream G650 touched down with elegant precision on the sleek tarmac of Le Bourget Airport, just past midnight. Paris shimmered in the distance, the Eiffel Tower a faint silhouette beneath a velvet sky. Victor Harrington stepped off the private jet with calm composure, dressed in a crisp charcoal coat, black gloves, and polished shoes that displayed elegance against the steps.

Waiting at the foot of the aircraft were five men dressed in tailored black suits, clearly from Silvio Arcuri's villa, their postures stiff and eyes colder than the night air. None of them spoke at first. But Victor noticed a flicker of familiarity in their expressions. They had seen him before. Years ago. Not in peace.

"Victor Harrington," one of them greeted finally. "Don Arcuri welcomes you to Paris."

Victor gave a slight nod, saying nothing. The moment was heavy—not with tension, but with unfinished business.

They led him silently to a matte-black Porsche Panamera parked just beyond the hangar lights. The

Parisian air carried a chill, but Victor moved calmly, his mind already rehearsing what needed to be said when he faced Silvio Arcuri—the man whose son he had nearly destroyed.

Victor reached for the car door, but something made him stop in his tracks.

Click. A gun cocked behind him, which was close. Too close.

Victor turned around slowly. Standing there was Gianni, clad in a dark overcoat, a silenced pistol aimed straight at his back. His face was tight with contempt, though a smug little smirk still crept through. "You didn't think you'd walk into Paris without paying what you owe to me?" Gianni sneered.

Victor didn't flinch. "I owe one man. And his name is Silvio, not you."

Gianni stepped forward. "Matteo was on the floor like a dying hound because of you. And you made me look foolish three times. Corsica. Palermo. Naples, too. I recall. Each and every fall."

Victor let out a slow breath, annoyed more than afraid. "I don't have time for this."

But Gianni's finger twitched near the trigger. The other four men took subtle steps outward, forming a loose circle around Victor.

"This isn't Silvio's command," Victor said, his voice now sharper. "You're doing this for yourself."

"Damn right," Gianni growled. "Silvio might listen to your pretty words, but I've waited too long for this."

Victor gave one last warning. "This was a mistake."

Then it took place. He moved quickly. An abrupt blur. Victor's right elbow cracked into Gianni's jaw while his left hand slammed the gun sideways before Gianni could fire. Gianni stumbled backward.

The other four were too slow in their instinctive reaction. Before driving his knee into the second man's chest, Victor dipped low and swept the legs from under him. Victor spun out and threw him face-first into the side mirror of the Porsche after a third seized him from behind. Victor grabbed his wrist in midair, shattered it cleanly with a single motion, and then pushed him into the asphalt. The fourth one had a blade.

Gianni lunged again, fury overtaking skill.

Victor halted him in his tracks and struck his ribs with his palm. With a crash that reverberated into the darkness, Victor ducked, seized Gianni's coat collar, and flung him into the sidewalk as he gasped and then swung blindly.

There were five bodies on the ground, moaning. Victor hardly appeared exhausted. After adjusting his coat, he looked at the dented mirror once before turning to face Gianni, who was attempting to crawl back up.

"This was your fourth mistake," Victor said coldly. "I won't be this polite the fifth time."

Victor stopped him in his tracks and struck his ribs with his palm. With a crash that reverberated into the darkness, Victor ducked, seized Gianni's coat collar, and flung him into the sidewalk as he gasped and then swung blindly. There were five bodies on the ground, moaning. Victor hardly appeared exhausted.

Victor opened the Porsche door, slid in, and started the engine. The roar of the V8 broke the silence, after straightening his coat, he looked at the dented mirror to see Gianni, who had been trying to crawl back up.

* * * *

# Chapter - 30

The Porsche raced along the north part of Paris, the engine steady under Victor's control. City lights dwindled in the rearview mirror, giving way to winding roads lined with tall trees and the occasional quiet, stone villa.

Victor's hands gripped the steering wheel, but his mind wasn't here, not on the road, not even in France. It was in Rome. It was in the night that never left him, ten Years Ago

* * * *

The night in Rome was thick with silence. No wind. No sirens. Just the faint buzz of electricity in the street lamps that cast long, trembling shadows across La Rosa Nera's villa.

Victor moved like a ghost. Dressed in black, his boots silent on the cobblestones, his eyes sharp as blades. He had already taken out the outer guards. Three men. Quick. Clean. No alarms. Their bodies rested behind hedges and marble statues, their weapons still warm.

The Villa stood before him. White stone, ivy-covered walls, the windows glowing with the calm light of home. Inside, Matteo Arcuri, the heir of La Rosa Nera. His friend.

Victor swallowed. He hadn't wanted this.

But Antonio Casella, the man who raised him, who carved him into a weapon, had made the order clear: "Kill Matteo. Then Silvio will learn his place. He's a threat to our expansion. Do it, and don't ask questions."

Victor never asked questions back then. He only followed orders. The door wasn't locked. That night, it never needed to be. Victor stepped inside. The marble floors felt cold beneath his boots. Paintings of saints and sinners lined the walls. The smell of wine, wood, and Roman pine lingered in the air.

In the study, he discovered Matteo, all alone. Gazing up from a leather chair with a cigarette in his right hand, the man smiled as he recognized the person. "Vic? What the hell, man—you didn't call." Matteo stood, surprised, but not alarmed. "Wait, is this one of those midnight Casella jobs again? Don't tell me you need me to go threaten that judge again."

Victor didn't smile.

He didn't move.

Matteo's grin faded. "Victor?"

Victor raised the pistol.

Matteo stepped back, confusion turning into fear. "You're kidding. Right? What is this?"

Victor's hands trembled, jaw locked tight.

"I'm sorry."

Three shots rang out.

Matteo collapsed against the bookshelves, blood staining the polished floor beneath him. He tried to speak, but only choked. Victor walked over, knelt beside him, his own eyes wet.

"You were my friend," he whispered. "You trusted me. And I abused that trust."

Footsteps echoed behind him. He turned and saw Silvio Arcuri standing at the entrance of the study, frozen, pale as stone. His eyes took in the scene: his son dead, Victor kneeling, pistol still in hand.

Victor's voice cracked. "You'll come for me, Silvio. Not today, maybe not even tomorrow. But you will. Because vengeance is the last refuge of the shattered. It gives purpose where love for a person used to live." Victor looked at Silvio, too shocked to understand what was going on.

"And when that day comes, I won't run. We both know this road ends with one of us in the ground. It's always been that way. "Victor said. "I'm sorry."

Then he dropped the gun. It hit the marble with a metallic thud.

Victor stood slowly, his knees weak, and walked past Silvio without another word. Silvio didn't move. Didn't speak. He only watched Victor vanish into the night, taking with him everything La Rosa Nera had once trusted.

That was the night La Rosa Nera abandoned Rome.

* * * * *

The memory faded as the Porsche turned past an old vineyard. Victor blinked back into the present, the pain in his chest returning like an echo.

Antonio had congratulated him on the killing. Victor hadn't spoken of the scream Matteo made, or the look in Silvio's eyes, the look of a father watching the world burn around him.

Now, ten years later, he was driving to that same father's doorstep. Victor slowed the car slightly and whispered to himself:

"Whatever happens next, I deserve it."

The gates of Villa Arcuri loomed ahead, tall and iron-wrought, flanked by men with rifles and stone faces. The Porsche rolled to a gentle stop near the long tree-lined driveway leading to the estate. The guards watched silently as Victor reached for his phone.

It was Cyrus.

Victor answered. "I'm nearly at Silvio's. If this is about the ambush earlier, I already dealt with it."

Cyrus's voice came through, calm but urgent. "No. This is about something else. Something bigger."

Victor's eyes narrowed. "Go on."

"You remember the Library of Secrets? The Grim Reaper had told you to find the key and the door too in order to get Vanessa from the Casellas."

Victor leaned back slightly, his pulse slowing. That name hadn't been uttered in days.

"I haven't forgotten," he said.

"I just sent the coordinates," Cyrus continued. "It's in Monte Carlo. Tucked beneath the old district. It matches what the Grim Reaper told us back in Whitechapel. And there's more—Marcus Volanti, head of the Volanti crime family in Monaco, coincidentally, he's holding the **key**. But he doesn't know what it unlocks. Or what it's worth."

Victor looked down at the notification on his screen. Coordinates. Monte Carlo. A red pin hovering over a stone-marked alley just behind the Grand Casino.

"I thought the key was lost. I made sure of that." Victor murmured.

"It was," Cyrus replied. "Until now. We traced an encrypted auction from six months ago. Marcus bought an artifact. Small. Black casing. 16<sup>th</sup> century symbol etched into the steel. It's the key, Victor. It has to be."

Victor stared out the windshield. Somewhere inside that villa waited Silvio Arcuri. A man ready to make him bleed for Matteo. And now, Monte Carlo was calling. A power none of the Five Pillars could afford to lose.

"You know what this means, right?" Victor said.

"I do," Cyrus replied. "The Library of Secrets isn't just a myth. If Volanti has the key and doesn't know it... we're running out of time."

Victor nodded slowly, already adjusting the route in his mind. "I'll handle Silvio first," he said. "Then I'll head to Monaco."

"You sure that's wise? You're walking into the lion's den."

Victor gave a tired smile. "Wouldn't be the first time."

He hung up. The guards stepped aside. The villa loomed ahead.

* * * *

# Chapter - 31

Victor walked alone through the towering iron gates of Silvio's villa. No rain tonight, only a dry Parisian wind and the low hum of cicadas beyond the hedges. The moon cast its pale glow on the pale stone villa, always cold, dignified, and cloaked in old ghosts. Two armed guards greeted him with blank stares.

"Weapons," one said.

Victor lifted his arms without protest. He had come unarmed, his blazer light, his hands empty. A long moment passed as they patted him down, twice. He knew the drill. They were more nervous than he was.

"You're clear," the second guard said. "Don Silvio is waiting."

They led him through the marbled halls into a lavish garden terrace, where a long table was set under glowing lanterns. Red wine, steaming dishes, fresh bread. And at the end of the table, dressed in an ivory blazer, sat Don Silvio Arcuri.

The man who once ruled Rome in shadows. Now exiled to Parisian luxury with vendetta in his veins.

Silvio stood and opened his arms with the grace of a viper. "Victor Harrington," he said. "You must be tired from the jet lag. And hungry after beating up my welcoming party at the airport."

Victor didn't sit. "I'm not hungry."

Silvio chuckled, a slow, dry laugh. "Gianni acted without my orders. I apologize. He's like a boy driven by emotion. Like Matteo once was."

Victor's eyes narrowed. "I didn't come here for your dogs. I came for you."

Silvio gestured toward the chair across from him. "Then sit. Speak. I assume this is not just a social visit."

Victor sat, but he didn't touch the wine or the warm bread before him. His voice was low, firm. "You should know, my son, Dante died two years ago."

Silvio's eyes flickered, just for a second. "So, now you think I understand your pain?"

Victor leaned forward slightly. "Now you understand mine."

Silvio fell silent.

Victor pressed on. "You lost Matteo. I lost Dante. Both of us bled for empires that broke us. But we still stand, Silvio. And we still have reasons to finish what we started."

Silvio looked away toward the garden hedges, where torches burned low.

Victor continued, steady and calm. "We unite. La Rosa Nera and what's left of me. We take down the Casellas. You get revenge for Rome. And I... I get Vanessa back. Away from their claws."

Silvio smiled, faintly, bitterly.

"I watched you kill my son," he said.

Victor's jaw tightened. "On orders. From Antonio Casella. I didn't want to. Matteo was my friend."

"Still, you did it," Silvio snapped.

Victor didn't flinch. "Because that was the world we belonged to."

A long pause. Then Silvio stood up slowly, brushing his coat sleeves. "You propose unity. But I offer you something simpler."

He snapped his fingers. Within seconds, the terrace was surrounded. Dozens of men, armed, masked, silent. Standing like shadows summoned by rage.

Victor stood slowly. He didn't reach for anything.

Silvio turned his back and walked toward the villa's doors. "No deal," he said. "You murdered my blood. I don't want allies. I want ashes."

Victor knew this would happen, and sighed. One of the guards tossed a velvet case at Victor's feet. It slid open to reveal two black pistols, polished and loaded. "Underworld law," the guard said. "We honor the enemy. You get to die fighting."

Victor bent down slowly, picked up the pistols. He nodded once. "Fair enough."

Then hell broke loose.

The first two attackers lunged, and soon Victor dropped one with a clean headshot, then pivoted and fired into the other's chest. Chaos erupted across the terrace. Gunfire flared. Men fell. Victor moved like a ghost with steel, fast and precise, but there were too many.

A rifle cracked. He spun. A blunt impact hit his ribs. Another kick to the back. Then darkness swallowed his vision.

He woke up coughing, his lungs stinging with smoke. He was lying in what used to be the Arcuri garden. Now it was fire and ruin. Flames clawed the villa walls. Stone cracked under heat. Blood painted the tiles near his feet— thick and fresh. His hands were soaked in it.

He stared at them in horror.

"Alexander..." Victor whispered. "Was this you?"

The voice echoed gently from within his mind. "Definitely not me, mate. But whatever happened, it wasn't small."

Victor staggered to his feet. The air reeked of blood and ash. There were no bodies left. Just scattered limbs, torn weapons, and heat. Somewhere in the chaos, Silvio ran, limping, bleeding, terrified. Victor followed without hesitation.

His boots crunched over broken tile and embers as he moved through the ruins like a shadow with purpose. Silvio stumbled into the courtyard, gasping, one hand pressed to his ribs. Victor closed the distance with ease.

"Silvio," he growled.

The man spun, eyes wild. "Victor—wait—"

Too late. Victor tackled him into the dirt. But the moment broke as three of Silvio's elite guards emerged from the smoke, rifles raised and trained on Victor's back.

Victor didn't flinch.

The first charged. Victor stepped into the blow, disarming him in a blur, cracking his skull against the edge of the shattered fountain. The second sprayed bullets blindly—Victor ducked, grabbed the man's wrist, and used his momentum to slam him into the garden wall. Bones shattered. The third managed a shot—grazing Victor's arm—before Victor rammed a broken shovel handle through his throat.

Blood soaked the soil.

Silvio tried to crawl away. Victor grabbed him by the collar, dragging him up, slamming him against the scorched statue of some long-dead Roman tyrant. "Do I need to remind you who I am?" Victor hissed.

Silvio choked, eyes wide. "You can't run from it... you can't bury your past, Victor. You can outrun the world, but never the version of yourself."

Victor's grip tightened.

"You're not Victor Harrington anymore. You're what they always feared. The Silent Ghost. You'll die in Paris, like a whisper lost in smoke. You'll never outrun the Five Pillars."

Victor didn't respond. He just snapped his neck. It was cold and necessary.

There was no time to grieve, no time to reflect. Not with the reinforcements storming through the gates, rifles drawn, shouting in Italian. The air thickened with the scent of gunpowder and vengeance.

But then the wind changed.

A roaring buzz ripped through the night sky as a black helicopter burst through the smoke clouds above. Its blades tore the fog open like a blade. A side panel slid open, revealing a mounted turret that wasted no time tearing into the approaching guards. Bullets shredded stone and bone alike.

A ladder dropped from the side.

Victor didn't hesitate. He sprinted, dodging gunfire, pain burning through his shoulder. He leapt, caught the swaying rungs, and climbed as the last of the gunmen were reduced to silence below.

Strong hands pulled him up. Inside, Cyrus stood grinning beneath a pair of black aviators, as calm as a man in peace.

"Not bad for a guy who said he was done with the field," Cyrus said, pushing the hatch shut behind them.

Victor collapsed into a seat, blood on his hands, smoke in his lungs. "You fly helicopters now?" he asked between breaths.

"I fly everything," Cyrus replied with a wink. "You just keep falling into hell and somehow climbing out. Told you Silvio won't work out."

Victor smirked, but his eyes were heavy. Tired. Haunted.

The city below faded beneath the clouds as the helicopter sped away from the wreckage of Paris. The fire was behind them. But the war?

"Where to?" Victor asked, wiping the blood from his forearm.

Cyrus adjusted the stick. "Monte Carlo, Monaco. There's Marcus there."

Victor leaned back in the seat, staring out at the stars breaking through the cloud line.

"Cyrus," Victor said, exhaling.

"Yeah mate?"

"We've got a hell of a lot of jobs to do."

* * * * *

The sea shimmered like molten silver beneath the sun as Victor Harrington rolled into Monte Carlo, his blue Peugeot rental driving through the winding coastal roads. Monaco was a city of money, masks, and monarchs in tuxedos. The kind of place where the people there wore cologne and secrets sparkled like diamonds.

Victor followed the exact directions Cyrus had sent—encrypted coordinates leading to a hilltop estate overlooking the city's glittering skyline, but he wasn't heading there, not yet, not directly.

His phone buzzed. Cyrus.

Victor answered, eyes still locked on the Riviera ahead. "Talk."

Cyrus's voice came crisp and low. "Marcus is throwing a gala tonight at the Orabella Estate. He's flaunting the key like a prize. It's on display, center stage. But Marcus still doesn't know what it is, only that it's old and valuable. If you take it quietly, without killing anyone, we can keep the Library of Secrets safe."

Victor tightened his grip on the steering wheel. "No blood?"

"None," Cyrus said. "Not tonight. We can't afford to let the Five Pillars get the key before you. If they see you, they'll come before you get there. Get in and get out in silence."

The line clicked off. Then a different voice chuckled inside Victor's mind.

"Oh, I quite like Monaco already."

Victor blinked, and a sudden chill rippled through his body. His hand trembled slightly—then stilled.

His reflection in the rearview mirror smiled back at him. Alexander. With a new confidence in his gait, Alexander tapped the steering wheel with rhythmic flair.

"Monte Carlo" he grinned. "Warm wind, elegant danger, and a gala with secrets? This is my kind of evening."

Victor's voice echoed faintly within. "Don't screw this up. No killing, remember."

Alexander smirked. "I'm not you. I don't have to kill to get what I want. Cheers to that."

He pulled into a discreet luxury hotel just off the Boulevard des Moulins. Valet in red. Doormen who didn't ask questions. The kind of place where men with pasts pretended they didn't have any pasts at all.

In the suite, that Alexander had booked, he stood before the mirror, rolling his shoulders, breathing deeply. The room smelled of old wood and rich perfume. He picked a suit, jet black tuxedo, silk-lined and no tie. Understated elegance. A charm.

He slipped on the silver cufflinks Cyrus had sent him—disguised transmitters if anything went wrong.

Victor's voice spoke again. "Don't lose control. The key matters more than us."

Alexander adjusted his collar. "Relax. Tonight, I am a gentleman. Also a thief in a ballroom."

He walked to the window and looked out toward the gleaming lights of the Orabella Estate, far above the glittering casinos and yachts below. Fireworks were already blooming in the sky over the Monte Carlo harbor.

A gala was waiting. And beneath all the champagne, silk gowns, and black-tie smiles was a key that could unlock a secret the world wasn't ready for.

Alexander grinned. "Let's go steal something beautiful."

* * * * *

T he hotel suite was soaked in soft gold light, with the glow of the setting sun spilling through the sheer curtains. Dressed in nothing but confidence, he ran a hand through his damp hair and smiled at his reflection in the tall mirror.

A devilish smile. Calm. Composed. Dangerous.

But then the sound of the television in the living area caught his attention.

"Breaking news. Interpol has issued a high-priority red notice for Victor Harrington, now a person of interest and currently missing. Sources close to Interpol believe he may be traveling under aliases across Europe and is in connection with the sudden disappearance of his wife, Vanessa Riva, a former political figure in London. Investigations reveal her last known location before vanishing was in Notting Hill, West London."

Alexander's smile faded as he walked over to the screen, still wrapped in the towel. On it flashed a grainy photo of him, taken from a traffic camera in Notting Hill weeks ago—face blurred, but still recognizable to the trained eye. A second image showed Vanessa, smiling warmly at a press event, frozen in time.

Alexander narrowed his eyes. "Of course," he muttered. "The past catches up quicker than the future."

Victor's voice echoed from deep within him, tired and subdued. "I didn't want this. I didn't want her caught in all this."

Alexander sighed and muted the television. "And yet, here we are."

Quickly, he dressed. The black tuxedo fit like a second skin. Shoes polished, cufflinks straightened. But as he glanced at himself one last time in the mirror, something felt off. Too familiar. Too traceable.

From the hotel lobby, he borrowed a simple black cap from the concierge's "Forgotten Items" box, which was something casual and something which lacked attention.

"Lost and found?" the clerk asked, raising an eyebrow.

"Found," Alexander replied with his head down and placing the cap over his head.

With one final glance at the shimmering city outside, Alexander left the hotel and slid into the rented Peugeot, parked in the underground lot. Not quite the Porsche, but subtle. Just what he needed.

Monte Carlo's streets buzzed with the energy of the night. Laughter from casinos. The soft roar of distant yachts. Tourists and moguls mingled like stars across the black velvet of the coast. But Alexander wasn't here to enjoy the scenery, although he wanted to.

"Victor... don't worry. I'll find the key. No blood. No bodies. Just masks, charm, and a little borrowed time."

Victor didn't respond.

And the silence felt heavier than the weight of a pistol. Tonight, in a palace of enemies, Alexander would be present there, and steal a secret the world had long forgotten.

*     *     *     *     *

# Chapter - 34

The Monte Carlo night gleamed like a gem, polished and proud. The Volanti estate sat high above the sea, wrapped in gold lighting and the sounds of string quartets and clinking champagne and the sound of flutes. From a distance, it looked like a palace built for gods. Up close, it was something else entirely, an opulence soaked in secrets.

The Peugeot pulled up just outside the marble steps. Alexander, draped in an elegant texture, stepped out and handed the valet the keys with the air of someone born to royalty. "All right, Victor," Alexander muttered, adjusting his bow tie as he walked up the steps, "let's just *pretend* we belong here among the millionaires and murderers."

Victor's voice stirred inside his head. "We do belong. Just not on the guest list."

Alexander smirked. "True. But Monte Carlo does love a little mystery."

He stepped through the grand entrance into a flood of warm light and orchestral strings. Crystal chandeliers sparkled above, refracting light onto the marble floors like shattered stars. Men in tailored suits and women in gowns that cost more than normal attires floated about with glasses of Dom Pérignon. Conversations ranged from art auctions to arms deals, veiled by laughter and expensive perfume.

Alexander made his way across the room, pausing at the edge of the balcony that overlooked the main gallery. "My, my," he murmured, leaning on the railing. "Look at the size of this place. Ever been in a hall this big, Victor?"

"Not unless it was burning down," Victor replied dryly.

Alexander chuckled in his usual soft British accent. "Well, let's try to leave this one standing, shall we?"

He descended the marble staircase into the heart of the gathering. Waiters glided past with silver trays; Alexander snatched a flute of champagne and sipped without a blink, walking as though he had always belonged.

Then he saw it.

Framed under a spotlight on a tall velvet pedestal behind tempered glass stood an artifact that looked ancient and unassuming: a brass key, aged with time, housed within a transparent dome. Small, ornate, with strange etchings along the stem. Latin. Ritualistic. Familiar.

The key to the Library of Secrets.

Alexander slowed his pace, keeping his eyes forward but glancing at it from the side. "There you are," he whispered under his breath.

Victor's voice echoed faintly. "It's real."

"Well, you were the one who lost it, mate. And unguarded, for now," Alexander replied. "But that won't last."

Just then, a waiter passed by and offered him an hors d'oeuvre. Alexander smiled politely, took one, then turned back toward the crowd, blending in again as a guest who was a well-dressed man enjoying the evening.

The orchestra began a soft tune. People moved toward the dance floor. But Alexander's eyes never left the key. People in elegant black and silver moved with the careful ease of wealth — and danger.

Victor, watching through Alexander's eyes, tensed for a moment.

"There," Victor said from deep within, guiding Alexander's gaze. "The one in the crimson dress. At the edge of the ballroom. Look at her posture which is not stiff like these socialites. She's scanning the room."

Alexander's eyes found her.

A woman, tall and poised, stood beside the bar with a glass of white wine untouched in her hand. Her crimson satin dress cut across her back and wrapped around her figure like fire. She had short, neat blonde hair tucked behind one ear, and her pale blue eyes — calm, sharp, cold — took everything in. She didn't belong, not truly. She pretended to. And that was dangerous.

"British," Alexander noted aloud. "Military background, from the way she holds her weight. You think she's Volanti's?"

"No," Victor answered. "She's not watching Marcus. She's watching the key. A friend of mine. Isabel Hart, former MI6. She is working with Cyrus. Go to her and ask for a dance. It'll blend you in."

Alexander hesitated. "You do remember you have a wife to rescue, right?"

Victor gave a dry chuckle in his mind. "This isn't about love. It's strategy. Trust me."

With a soft sigh, Alexander smoothed his tuxedo, adjusted the cufflink, and stepped forward.

As he approached, the woman looked up, her expression unreadable. A flicker of something crossed her face somewhat of recognition, relief or even maybe confusion.

"Victor Harrington," she said with a trace of disbelief, her accent crisp London. "Well, you're late."

Alexander blinked. She knew Victor. But not *him*. He offered a smooth smile, his voice calm. "You look like someone expecting more blood and less ballroom."

She cracked the faintest grin. "Maybe both. Come." Without waiting, she pulled him gently to the floor, joining the others already moving to a sultry waltz.

"Why are you here?" Alexander asked, already knowing the answer.

"Same as you. The key." Her eyes darted past his shoulder. "But I'm not here to steal it. I'm here to make sure you do. Alone."

Alexander narrowed his eyes. "You're not helping?"

"No one can help you with this," Isabel said quietly. "Cyrus made that very clear. The key must be taken by your hands. Not stolen, not handed, not traded. Taken. You have one window, Victor. One shot. Also, it is your time to get back at the world."

Her voice turned lower, harsher. "Get it. And get out. If you fail, Marcus will destroy you."

Alexander gave a slow nod. "Does Cyrus know you're here?" he asked. He needed to control himself from asking obvious questions. Inside his head, Victor's voice was quiet now, listening.

Isabel nodded once. "He trusted me to pass the message. And to watch you. He said you'd try to do something reckless. Like killing someone."

She leaned close. "Don't. Not tonight. If you do, the Pillars will know. The Library of Secrets must stay silent, or the underworld will never be balanced. Not that they are balanced now."

The music surged into its final refrain. Alexander spun her once, then steadied her in place. The antique clock high on the wall ticked toward midnight. The key sat across the room, behind its pristine glass.

The countdown had begun. The clock struck midnight.

The waltz ended with a thunderous silence, followed by polite claps. Then came the quiet — the kind that settles before a storm.

Alexander stood at the edge of the display. Victor whispered inside him. "It's the real one. No decoy. Take it now."

Alexander looked around. The security near the key had thinned. Guests wandered back toward the champagne fountains. Isabel had vanished into the crowd, exactly as a ghost like she would.

With a quiet breath, Alexander stepped forward. His cufflink flickered once, indicating a signal from Cyrus.

Now. He slid a narrow tool from the inside of his sleeve. One twist. One lift. The glass came loose in his hands like it was begging to be taken. He reached in and his fingers brushed the metal. The next moment, the chandeliers exploded in sparks. Gunshots.

Screams pierced the air as a dozen masked mercenaries in matte-black gear stormed the ballroom, weapons raised, voices shouting commands in different languages. The crowd erupted into chaos, high heels scattering across marble, guards diving for cover.

Alexander ducked, the key gripped tight in his fist.

Victor's voice surged, sharp and alert. "Five Pillars. I recognize their emblem, right shoulder patch. The Casellas leads them."

Suddenly, sirens. Blue and red lights danced across the stained-glass windows. Outside, Monaco's police swarmed the entrance, barking orders, guns drawn.

And then, came the command. "Victor Harrington! Hands where we can see them!"

Alexander cursed under his breath. "We're boxed in."

"Airport," came Cyrus's voice suddenly through the cufflink. Calm. Icy. "Ride soon. The jet is waiting. Get the key to Rome. No deviations."

Alexander turned back, and saw Isabel standing by a shattered pillar, her arm grazed, blood on her dress.

He ran to her, grabbing her arm.

"You need to go. Disappear. Now."

She gave him a fierce look. "No would be the answer."

"It's suicide here".

"Go, Victor. I'll cover you." Isabel told Alexander.

Alexander ran. Through fire, broken crystal and screams that came from the hall. He burst through a side exit, racing through the garden maze toward the back gates. His blue Peugeot rental waited behind the hedge, still humming. Alexander forgot to turn it off. He cursed himself.

He jumped in, slammed the door, tires screeching as he pulled into the back street and merged into traffic, sirens echoing behind him.

Inside, Victor was quiet. Then he spoke. "They're all watching now. Every Pillar. Every government. They all want it. Seems like they know of the key's existence."

Alexander looked down at the key beside him on the seat. Ancient. Small. And yet — unbearably heavy.

"Rome next," he muttered. He floored the gas. Alexander gripped the steering wheel of the Peugeot, weaving through the narrow roads of Monte Carlo. Behind him, red and blue lights flashed violently. Police cars howled after him like wolves in uniform. Worse still, three matte-black SUVs surged through traffic, their tinted windows hiding the mercenaries of the Five Pillars.

Victor's voice sparked from within. "Can't you get the car faster? You know that if we go in this pace, we'll never make it in time."

Alexander smirked. "Not with me behind the wheel." He yanked the steering hard, cutting through a small roundabout, nearly missing a delivery truck. Tires screeched. The Peugeot lunged forward with everything it had, darting past astonished drivers.

But behind him, the black SUVs weren't giving up. One pulled up beside him, windows lowering, and an assault rifle emerged.

"Ah, hell—" Alexander ducked just as a bullet cracked through the back window.

* * * *

# Chapter - 35

Back at the half-destroyed villa, Isabel picked up her phone, voice sharp and low. "Cyrus. It's me."

"Status?" came his reply.

"Victor has the key. The Five Pillars and Monaco PD are chasing him. I need Inferno deployed."

A pause. Then Cyrus spoke. "It'll be done."

Smoke still curled into the starless sky as Marcus stepped out of the armored vehicle, his leather shoes crunching against the gravel and ash. The once-glorious Volanti villa lay in charred ruins, cracked marble, shattered glass, and the burnt scent of betrayal lingering in the air.

His eyes scanned the wreckage, expression unreadable, jaw tense.

"The key is gone," one of his guards said grimly. "Inferno did this."

Marcus narrowed his eyes. "No, not Inferno alone." He turned toward the distant hills, his voice low and venomous. "She helped them. Isabel."

He took a breath, slow and controlled. "Bring her in. Alive."

Moments later, in a secluded chamber beneath one of Marcus' hidden compounds, Isabel sat bound to a velvet chair, her lip bloodied, her dress torn at the shoulder.

Marcus stood in front of her, calm as ever, a glass of bourbon in his hand.

"You helped them escape," he said.

"You gave them my key. And now, I'll trade you for it."

Isabel didn't flinch. "You won't get it. He's long gone."

Marcus leaned forward, his voice a serpent's hiss. "You've always been clever. But clever women can still bleed."

She smiled through bruised lips. "So can arrogant men."

Suddenly, the lights flickered. Gas hissed. A flash-bang erupted behind Marcus.

By the time he turned around, coughing, blinded, Isabel had slipped her cuffs, disarmed the guard beside her, and kicked Marcus back into the wall.

She ran through the corridor as alarms blared. As guards gave chase, she disappeared through a maintenance hatch into the night.

Marcus, rising from the ground, shouted after her with cold fury. "Run as far as you like, Isabel. I will burn every city to find you or Victor. And I will get that key."

But she was already gone.

* * * * *

# Chapter - 36

The Peugeot's engine screamed through the narrow veins of Monte Carlo as Alexander slammed the gearstick, tires screeching against cobblestone. Streetlights whipped past in golden blurs. Sirens blared behind him, multiplying like a pack of hounds with teeth made of steel.

"Left," Victor's voice said from the back of his mind.

Alexander cut the wheel hard, the car drifting sideways through a cramped intersection, knocking over café tables and narrowly missing a delivery bike that swerved into a fruit stand. Oranges exploded into the air like shrapnel. A police cruiser clipped the edge of the same corner and spun out, slamming into a parked Mercedes.

"Oops," Alexander grinned, wiping blood from his lip.

But there was no time for apology. Three more police vehicles chased close behind, their flashing lights bouncing off polished storefronts. And farther back, more dangerous than the police, were black unmarked SUVs, fast and merciless, filled with Five Pillars mercenaries, armed to the teeth.

Automatic fire cracked against the Peugeot's rear. The back window shattered. Glass rained inside.

"Faster," Victor urged.

"Working on it," Alexander hissed, slamming the accelerator.

He weaved the Peugeot down a tight alley that looked too narrow to fit a car, skimming within inches of brick walls, sparks flying as side mirrors scraped stone. One police car tried to follow. It got halfway before its front bumper slammed into a dumpster, flipping the car in a crunch of metal.

Alexander burst out the other end, tires catching air off a curb and landing with a jolt. The Peugeot bounced once, then surged forward toward the coast road—a ribbon of highway dangling above the cliffs.

From above, a drone buzzed. Red laser dots flickered briefly on the windshield.

"Sniper drone," Victor warned. "Low and left. Now!"

Alexander jerked the wheel. The shot fired. A hole tore through the hood, but missed the engine block by inches.

With no hesitation, he yanked the handbrake and spun the car into a 180 drift, reversing down the hill for a second before slamming it back into drive. He cut through a plaza filled with dancers and tourists. Screams erupted. Tables flipped. He swerved again, this time using a marble statue as cover from the drone above. The bullet that followed exploded the statue's head instead.

Then came the SUV. It roared up beside him, window down, mercenary aiming an Uzi out the side.

"Now this is getting really personal to me. I hate cars getting more damaged." Alexander muttered.

He jerked the car into the SUV's path, clipping the side. The mercenary opened fire and bullets tore through the passenger side door. Alexander swerved toward a construction ramp. Victor shouted: "Do it."

Alexander gritted his teeth, and launched the Peugeot into the air.

Time slowed.

The car soared over a parked city tram, cleared a construction crane, and landed with a sickening crunch on the other side, which resulted in destroying a hot dog stand and smashing the suspension. He didn't stop.

The SUV behind tried the same move, but clipped the crane. The vehicle exploded mid-air in a rolling fireball. Police sirens faded behind him, but more black bikes and jeeps cut through from the coast, blocking the next tunnel.

Suddenly, the sky thundered. A black helicopter burst through the clouds—silent at first, until its rotor wind blasted the street. Twin cannons swiveled into place.

Boom.

The first jeep exploded in a pillar of fire. The bikes scattered, two crashing into the guardrails. The chopper descended lower, and a metallic rope ladder unfurled.

Alexander skidded the Peugeot to a stop, kicked open the door, and sprinted toward the swinging rope.

Bullets peppered the pavement around him, but he leapt—catching the ladder mid-air.

As the helicopter lifted, he climbed fast, boots slipping on the cord. Below, fire engulfed the road. The city shrank beneath him.

A hand reached down from the open hatch.

"About time," Alexander grunted, grabbing it.

"Don't thank me," said Cyrus, pulling him in with ease. "Just tell me where you learned to drive like that."

Alexander collapsed onto the floor of the chopper, laughing breathlessly. "Let's just say... Victor had a few joyrides in his past life."

Cyrus grinned. "Well, Monaco's going to hate us."

Alexander looked out the hatch one last time. The city lights flickered behind smoke and sirens. "I did it for something right."

Alexander let out a tired grin and collapsed into the plush leather seat. "Your turn. I'm done for now."

And just like that, Victor Harrington was back in the game.

* * * * *

# Chapter - 37

Elsewhere, the Casella villa in Rome was a fortress dressed in vast elegance and luxury. The scent of jasmine floated through the air, carried by the breeze from the manicured gardens beyond the barred windows. But for Vanessa, there was no beauty in this place, but only ghosts of Victor's past.

She sat still on the velvet chaise, hands resting gently on her lap. Beneath her calm was a fire she refused to show—not to them.

The heavy door groaned open. Footsteps echoed, deliberate and sharp.

Giovanni Casella entered first, with his expression unreadable, suit crisp, posture regal. Beside him, Leonardo, Casella, younger and sharper, with a style that always tried too hard to mimic his father's cruelty.

Giovanni's voice was calm as he crossed the room. "The pieces I had set up for Victor have moved perfectly. He walks straight into our plans."

Leonardo chuckled. "He's brought us the key. And dismantled our enemies without knowing whose hand he truly plays for." He looked to Vanessa. "We'll open the door to the Library of Secrets soon, under the Cathedral of Florence."

Vanessa slowly looked up, her eyes meeting Giovanni's with a fierce, quiet rage. "He's coming for you."

Giovanni's brows furrowed slightly, but he said nothing.

Vanessa stood, the dim light casting long shadows behind her. "Victor made a vow. If he ever returned to Rome, he wouldn't leave until you were both dead." Her voice was low and steady. "He would bring fire to this villa. Stone by stone, it will fall."

Leonardo's grin faltered.

But she wasn't finished. "And Dante's death." her voice dipped, emotion flickering just beneath. "Will be avenged. Victor will tear down the Five Pillars. One by one. And he'll start with the you and your empire that you had built."

The air thickened. Even the guards outside the door shifted.

Giovanni's jaw tensed. His silence was louder than anything Leonardo could mock. Without another word, the Casella brothers turned and left the room, locking the door behind them.

Vanessa exhaled slowly. She turned toward the window, moonlight spilling across the floor.

"Come back to me, Victor," she whispered. "And let them feel what it means to lose everything."

* * * * *

# Chapter – 38

The private jet touched down at Rome Ciampino Airport just as the moon was in the sky, casting a dark surrounding over Rome. It was fitting, Victor thought, as he stepped out of the cabin and felt the cold wind press against his face.

The city stretched out beyond the tarmac like a sleeping beast—silent, old, unforgiving. Victor stepped off the aircraft, cold wind curling through his coat. He didn't flinch.

Rome was not a city. Not to him. Instead, it was a graveyard of memories dressed in gold. As his boots struck the stone-paved runway, the world tilted—softened—and flickered.

Then came the memories. The memories he kept in his mind year ago.

* * * * *

The marble floors were cracked and cold beneath his feet. He was ten, barefoot, panting, a wooden training blade slick with sweat in his grip. Blood trickled from a fresh cut along his cheek. His lungs ached, but he didn't stop running.

"Don't run, Victor," Antonio Casella's voice thundered across the courtyard. "Stand and fight like a man."

Victor stopped. Not out of courage, but fear. That particular kind of fear only Antonio could command. He turned, breath sharp and shallow, and raised his blade. Victor wanted to learn that fear which his father had.

Antonio stepped into the moonlight with a slow, deliberate stride. He wasn't just a father, but he was a tyrant draped in elegance. He wore a tailored suit, hands clasped behind his back, like he was conducting a lesson, not breaking a child.

"You hesitate," Antonio said, circling him. "And hesitation is weakness. What do we do with weakness?"

Victor whispered, "We cut it out."

"Good," Antonio said flatly. "Now again."

They clashed. Wooden blades snapping through the air. Antonio moved like a phantom. Victor, smaller, desperate, struck high. But Antonio parried with ease and knocked him flat onto the stone. The breath flew out of his lungs. Pain bloomed in his ribs.

"You'll never survive this world with a conscience," Antonio muttered, crouching beside him. "Mercy is a leash. And I didn't raise a pet. Grow up Victor."

Victor said nothing. He couldn't. Antonio leaned in closer, his voice like ice. "You want to live? Then forget who you are. Become what I need."

* * * * *

The present snapped back like a rubber band.

Victor blinked. The runway returned. The cold wind pressed against his back once more. But the weight of the past stayed lodged in his bones.

He looked out across the Roman skyline—ancient domes, broken statues, and towers standing like sentinels to old sins. The city of blood oaths and broken promises. The city he swore never to return to unless it was to burn it down.

He was no longer the boy with the blade. He was the man returning to finish what the boy never could. And this time, mercy would not be in his hands.

Waiting at the foot of the stairs was Cyrus. His overcoat billowed lightly in the breeze, and his face was calm, but his eyes carried a thousand unspoken operations. He looked up at Victor and smiled faintly.

"Welcome back to the graveyard, Victor," Cyrus said.

Victor didn't smile. His eyes drifted across the skyline, catching the distant glow of the ancient city. "Tell me it's ready."

Cyrus nodded. "The Inferno mercenaries are stationed in the hills outside the Casella villa. When we give the signal, they move in, eliminate all threats, and extract Vanessa safely."

Victor turned, adjusting the collar of his black coat. His voice was colder than the Roman dusk. He changed his mind. "No. I'll go in first."

Cyrus raised a brow. "Victor—"

"I'm not here for extraction. I'm here for reckoning." Victor's voice sharpened with fury. "Giovanni and Leonardo Casella murdered my son. They made me watch my family bleed. They destroyed Dante. For that... I will not give them the mercy of death by a soldier's bullet. I will burn them myself."

Cyrus exhaled, then nodded solemnly. "And the Grim Reaper?"

Victor's gaze darkened. "When I find him, I'll drag him into the shadows he crawled from. And I'll kill him too."

The two men received a briefcase. Inside a matte-black case, the metal Key to the Library of Secrets shimmered under the interior light.

Victor picked it up carefully. "This," he said, "must never fall into their hands."

He opened the second compartment of the case, where a decoy identical to the real key had been crafted by

Inferno's finest forgers. Victor turned to a stocky man in black military gear standing nearby—a hardened Inferno lieutenant with the emblem of the burning wolf on his shoulder.

"Take the real key," Victor ordered. "Secure it inside the Inferno bunkers in Spain. Deep within the vault. Not even Cyrus will know its location. This is my order."

The man nodded and disappeared into a separate vehicle, speeding off into the dark.

Victor now turned back to the car, which was sleek and scarlet red. A Ferrari 812 Superfast, gifted to him long ago by a syndicate boss, was now restored and returned to him by Inferno's network in Italy.

He slid into the driver's seat. Cyrus sat beside him. As the engine roared to life, Victor's hands gripped the wheel tightly, and his mind began to drift.

To the past. The gunfire. The betrayal. The broken voice of Antonio, bleeding out beside him, whispering, "Don't come back here... not unless it's to finish them."

The faces of his two brothers twisted with greed, ambition, and cruelty.

The silence of his son's empty room. Victor blinked back the memories. He wasn't that broken man anymore. He was the storm that followed.

"Let's end this."

He slammed the pedal down.

The Ferrari raced across the Roman hills, toward the Casella villa—toward vengeance, fire, and blood.

* * * * *

# Chapter - 39

Years ago, in Rome, the night reeked of cigar smoke, expensive betrayal, and something colder than death.

Victor stood in the courtyard of the Casella villa. The moonlight bathed the marble steps in pale silver. The fountain gurgled peacefully behind him, but his heart was hammering like a war drum.

Gunshots and screams were heard. Then followed silence. Victor ran.

Inside the villa, the air was heavy with gunpowder and cologne. Servants were gone. Curtains fluttered like ghosts. And at the center of the grand hall, laid face-down in a pool of blood, was Antonio, the patriarch of the Casella Empire. His tailored suit torn. His ringed hand limp.

Victor froze. He had left his father for only ten minutes.

Victor had spent most of his youth resenting his father, not for his power, but for his distance. Antonio was a man carved from stone. He was cold, calculating, and brutally disciplined. He had raised Victor not with affection, but with expectation, demanding strength, silence, and strategy.

And yet, despite the resentment, Victor couldn't deny the strange reverence he felt. Antonio was everything the world feared and respected. Elegant in chaos and regal in violence. In his own way, the old man had shaped Victor into someone who could survive the cruel world. As much as he had hated the shadows of his upbringing, Victor still admired the man behind the empire. Because beneath the hard silence and the empire's cruelty, Antonio had never once betrayed his blood.

A cold voice behind him sliced through the air like a blade. "He gasped your name before he died."

Victor turned, fists clenched. From the shadows emerged a man in black, his face masked, his presence like death itself. The myth whispered across Europe... The Four Horsemen...The Grim Reaper.

"Who sent you?" Victor barked, fury rising.

"I'll give you one guess," the Reaper replied coolly.

Then Victor saw it.

In the man's gloved hand: a silver Casella seal — one only the brothers could access.

Victor's heart dropped. "Leonardo and Giovanni."

They had done it. They had murdered their own father. For the empire. For the crown.

"You traitorous dog!" Victor roared and charged at the assassin.

He threw the first punch, raw and explosive. The Reaper staggered back, but regained balance immediately. Victor came at him again, fists like fire, fury in every blow. He slammed the man into the pillar, punched his jaw, kicked him in the ribs. Years of street fights, every form of training, and his life lessons all came back in an explosion of vengeance.

But the Grim Reaper wasn't an ordinary killer. In one sweeping move, the assassin twisted Victor's arm, spun him off balance, and sent him crashing into a glass cabinet.

Victor rolled and came up bleeding.

The Reaper stepped forward, silent and methodical.

Another swing was blocked.

A strike to Victor's ribs was made brutal.

Then the butt of the Reaper's gun hit Victor square in the temple. He crashed to the marble floor, vision spinning, blood soaking the collar of his shirt.

Through the haze, he saw the assassin standing over him.

"You're strong," the Reaper said. "But strength is nothing without purpose."

He knelt beside Victor and whispered, "When you find your purpose, Harrington... I'll be waiting."

And then he was gone, vanished into the shadows like smoke.

Victor lay there, broken and bleeding beside his father's corpse, the weight of betrayal crushing him. That was the night something inside him died.

* * * *

# Chapter - 40

The moon hung low over the outskirts of Rome, casting a silver gleam across the once-pristine Casella villa, now a den of crime. The guards were everywhere, patrolling the balconies, the courtyards, the long marble halls that once echoed with family dinners and wine-soaked laughter. It wasn't a home anymore. It was a fortress. A mausoleum of treachery.

From a hidden alcove near the northern wall, Victor stood still, face cold and unreadable. The wrought-iron gate had already closed behind him. His coat swayed in the breeze as he handed a steel case back to Cyrus.

"Stay here," Victor said quietly. "No matter what you hear. I'm finishing this."

Cyrus nodded without a word. He knew the look in Victor's eyes, the one that meant death was coming.

Victor unlatched the case and pulled out two weapons. A customized Glock 19 with a red-dot sight, and a hand-forged combat knife with a blackened hilt. The knife gleamed as he slid it across his forearm, checking the weight. The moment was still. Silent. Sacred.

Then he moved.

The first two guards didn't even hear him coming. A snap of the silencer and two neat shots went straight through their eyeballs, skulls cracking like porcelain as they dropped in tandem beside the garden hedges. Victor stepped over their corpses without a glance.

Another pair turned the corner. One barely had time to gasp before Victor's knife sliced across his throat in a clean, diagonal arc. The second lunged forward with a stuttered cry, only to be caught mid-motion. Victor drove the blade under his jaw, upward into the base of the skull. The man twitched, gurgled, and dropped.

Victor stormed the inner corridor.

A guard rushed him with a shotgun. Victor ducked beneath the barrel, twisted the man's wrist until it shattered with a pop, then shoved the muzzle against the man's gut and pulled the trigger. Blood and bits of intestine splattered the nearby wall. Before the body hit the ground, Victor was already moving.

A hail of bullets came from the staircase. He dove behind the marble pillar, rolled, then popped out and fired three precise shots. One hit the knee. The guard screamed, falling forward. Another shot took out his shoulder, spinning him around. The final one entered through the cheek, snapping the jawbone sideways as the man collapsed, convulsing.

Victor was no longer a man. He was a machine in motion.

He reached the grand hall, the place where he once celebrated his good days. Now, past memories painted the white walls.

Two more guards charged from opposite ends. Victor pivoted, fired one shot to the right, a headshot that snapped the man's neck backward with a gruesome crunch. The second raised his rifle, but Victor threw his knife—spinning through the air, and it lodged deep into the man's sternum. The impact knocked him flat against the floor.

Victor ran up and stomped on the man's chest, shattering ribs. Then he pulled the blade free, dragging it across the guard's face. The screams echoed briefly, then were silenced.

One final hallway led to the inner chambers.

Victor's eyes narrowed. Two more henchmen were there in front of him.

The first one swung wildly. Victor blocked with his forearm, ignoring the pain, then elbowed the man's throat and shoved his knife into the soft part under the ribcage. He twisted it hard, breaking bone, cutting into the liver. The man gasped and collapsed.

The second tackled Victor into the wall, jabbing with the stun baton. Electricity surged, but Victor grabbed the man's wrist, slammed his head into the wall twice—bone cracking—and then shoved his thumb into the guard's eye socket. He screamed. Victor twisted deeper until the eyeball burst with a wet *pop*, and the man slumped down, twitching.

Breathing heavily, covered in blood, in his own and others', Victor stood in the middle of the ruined hallway.

* * * * *

# Chapter - 41

At the far end, Giovanni Casella stood with a pistol pressed hard against Vanessa's temple. Her wrists were tied, but her eyes—those fierce, unbreakable eyes were locked onto Victor the moment he entered.

Leonardo stood beside Giovanni, hands clasped nervously. No gun. No plan. Just arrogance. "Drop your weapons, Victor," Giovanni said with a sneer. "Toss the key. Or she dies."

Victor's eyes didn't move from Vanessa's.

"I'm not here to gamble," Giovanni growled. "Give. Me. The key."

Victor raised his hand slowly and tossed the small obsidian-colored key toward them. Giovanni caught it mid-air, his attention momentarily stolen by the very thing he'd spent years chasing.

And in that single heartbeat of distraction, Victor moved. One clean shot.

*CRACK!*

Giovanni screamed, dropping the gun as blood burst from his shattered hand. Vanessa lunged away and ran into Victor's arms, collapsing into him as he shielded her with his body.

Leonardo backed up, trembling. "You're mad, Victor. This—this is not how it was supposed to end—"

Victor didn't respond. He raised his gun, aiming it straight at the two men who stole everything from him. But just as he pulled the trigger—

*WHAM!*

A black figure crashed into Victor from behind, sending him sprawling across the floor.

The Grim Reaper had arrived. Clad in a dark exo-suit, the figure moved like a shadow and death itself. His boot slammed into Victor's ribs, then another blow cracked his jaw. He kicked the gun away.

"You think this is over, Victor?" the Reaper growled. "No. I still have a score to settle. For the night at Rome. For what you did to me. For the blood trail you left behind."

Victor coughed blood, groaning in agony. His ribs were fractured, muscles torn. He could barely move. The Reaper grabbed him by the neck and slammed him into the stone wall. The impact cracked the plaster behind him.

Everything began to fade. Darkness crept in. And then... a voice.

Soft. Calm. Familiar. Dante.

Victor closed his eyes—and there he was. His son. Young. Smiling. Innocent. A memory preserved in light. "Don't let this be the end, Dad," Dante said gently. "You're not done yet. Don't let the ones who killed me and grandfather win. Stand up. Do what you need to do."

Victor's eyes snapped open.

He caught the Reaper's wrist mid-strike. With a guttural roar, he twisted it—CRACK! —shattering the bones like dry wood. The Reaper staggered back, screaming. Victor rose like a resurrected god of vengeance.

He unleashed a brutal storm of punches—one to the gut, another to the jaw, a third straight to the temple. The Reaper buckled under the weight of every strike. Each blow echoed with rage, grief, and fire. "You killed Dante," Victor said, voice trembling with fury. "You pulled the trigger. You took my father!"

He grabbed the Reaper by the collar and tore the mask off.

Everyone froze. It wasn't a stranger. It was Matteo. Matteo Arcuri. Victor's old ally. His old friend.

Victor stumbled back, heart cracking wide open. "Matteo...?"

Matteo coughed blood and gave a tired smile. "The night you thought you killed me... that wasn't me. Silvio knew what was coming. He placed a doppelgänger in my stead. He always had contingency plans."

Victor's voice was a whisper. "You were working for your father all along?"

Matteo slowly shook his head. "No, Victor. I was working for anyone who comes upto me to for a kill. When I had the chance to kill your son, I took it. Because deep inside, I despised you. You were never my friend, Victor. You had won all the fame, glory and the legend of the Underworld, while I was proclaimed dead, and had to operate under a mask."

Victor froze.

Matteo continued, pain etched into every word. "I loved him Antonio like you did. He saved me. He gave me a reason to live when I had none. When he died... I broke. I let my soul rot. And when my father offered me a way back, by putting on a mask, I thought, maybe, just maybe, I could find justice in a different form. But it was a lie."

Victor's fists trembled. "Then why wear the mask?"

"Because I couldn't face you," Matteo said, eyes cold. "I couldn't face the man who still had hope. You lost your son and your father through my hands. And still, you chose the fire of justice. And I became the ash. Or the leftovers."

Victor's voice cracked. "You should have told me."

Matteo smiled weakly. "Would you have listened? Or would you have pulled the trigger?"

Silence fell between them.

Victor looked at him—really looked—and saw the years, the guilt, the weight Matteo had carried. "Antonio would've forgiven you," Victor said finally. "But I'm not Antonio." He raised the gun.

Matteo nodded. "I know. And I'm not asking for mercy."

BANG. BANG. BANG.

Victor emptied the magazine. The man he once called friend collapsed in a pool of red—quiet, still, at peace.

Victor stood there, chest heaving, broken again.

Behind him, Giovanni whimpered, holding his mangled hand. Leonardo tried to crawl away like a rat in the shadows.

Victor turned, face unreadable.

"You should've never come for me," he said softly. "You should've never touched Dante. Matteo listened to both of you to kill my son. Because now…"

He raised the gun.

BANG. Giovanni dropped, a hole between his eyes.

Leonardo looked shocked. He crawled back, dragging himself backwards. "You think this ends with me?" he snarled, gasping. "You think killing us brings peace? You're a fool, Victor. I was just one piece on the board."

Victor didn't respond. His silence was heavier than words.

Leonardo's eyes darted toward Vanessa. "There are four more. Four more pillars. Four more shadows darker than me. Smarter. Crueler. And now that I'm gone, they'll come. From every corner of the world. No matter where you hide. No matter who you're with. They'll hunt you. And her. They'll make you watch her die. And when they do… you'll beg for death."

Victor stepped forward, his gun steady, his voice like steel. "Let them come," he said coldly. "I've buried and killed people. Burned places. Watched my own blood spill across cold floors like this one. I've walked through hell, and I didn't flinch."

He leaned in, lowering his voice to a deathly whisper. "You hide your heart behind your kills. That doesn't make it bulletproof. Any man who dares knock on my door, should better bloody bring an army. Because I won't be hiding. I'll be waiting."

Then, with one final breath, he pulled the trigger—BANG—and Leonardo's body hit the ground like a crumpled memory. But it wasn't over. Victor walked to their corpses and began kicking. Bones cracked. Blood spattered. He screamed their names. Screamed Dante's. Screamed Antonio's. Screamed his own.

Until Vanessa ran in, tears in her eyes. "Victor. Stop. Please."

He froze. His hand was trembling, covered in blood. Victor let out a bitter breath. "What I did here, it wasn't justice. It wasn't redemption. It wasn't even closure."

"Then what was it?" she asked, softly.

Victor looked toward the bodies. Then back at her. "It was retribution. For every lie. For every scar. For every scream that was buried in silence. And if more come for me... then let them. I'll stand. I'll fight. Because I've already walked through hell—and I didn't come back for mercy. Or forgiveness."

Vanessa slowly pulled him into an embrace. He collapsed into her, sobbing, broken, shivering.

* * * *

# Chapter - 42

Two months later

The bell above the bookstore door chimed softly as Victor turned the sign to *Closed*. Outside, the sun was beginning to set. One of those quiet golden evenings that made Notting Hill feel like a place untouched by the world's violence. Inside, the scent of old paper and roasted coffee lingered, mingling with the low hum of a vinyl record spinning in the corner.

Victor moved with a slower rhythm now. He shelved a few last books, ran a cloth along the counter, and took a moment to just breathe. The chaos was behind him—gunfire and bloodshed. All of it buried beneath cobblestone streets and unmarked graves.

Vanessa entered through the back, her hair tied in a loose bun, still wearing the black apron from her shift at the bar down the street. "Long day?" she asked with a soft smile.

Victor returned it. "Some tourist tried to tell me Shakespeare was not a good man. I nearly threw Hamlet at his head."

She laughed, came close, wrapped her arms around him from behind. "That's why I love you. Always a little dramatic."

He leaned into her touch, letting the comfort of her presence ground him. For the first time in years, the silence didn't feel empty. It felt earned.

Vanessa worked evenings and mornings as a bartender, always home by midnight. Victor opened the shop in the morning, read during the slow hours, and sometimes watched the rain without saying a word.

And yet, in all this peace, there was one voice that hadn't spoken in two months. Alexander.

Victor often sat on the edge of his bed at night, listening. Waiting. But the voice never returned. No soft encouragement. No haunting memories. Just silence.

Maybe he was finally at rest. Or maybe Victor had finally let himself enough to let him go.

As they stood together watching the sun dip behind the buildings, Vanessa whispered, "Do you miss it? That life?"

Victor didn't answer right away. He looked at her, at the soft glow in her eyes, at the safety he'd never thought he'd find again.

"No," he said at last. "The only thing I miss is that not finding this peaceful life sooner."

She kissed him gently on his cheek. Two souls who had been broken had somehow found each other again.

And in that quiet little corner of Notting Hill, among books and bottles and the soft rustle of the wind, Victor Harrington found something rarer than revenge. He had found peace.

* * * *

*Epilouge*

The city hummed faintly in the distance, but here, among the rows of stone and silence, it felt like time stood still. The wind carried a softness, like a lullaby for the departed at Highgate Cemetery.

Victor stood with one hand in his coat pocket, the other holding a small bouquet of blue forget-me-nots. Vanessa stood beside him, wrapped in a long beige coat, her scarf fluttering against her chest.

Victor knelt slowly besides his son's grave, and placed the flowers at the base of the stone. His hand lingered there, fingertips tracing the carved letters. "He would've been eight last week," he said softly, voice thick but calm. "He used to say he'd be a knight. Or a poet. Or both."

Vanessa smiled gently, eyes glistening. "He said he'd protect the world from monsters," she whispered. "And carry a sword made of fire. His imagination was way different from ours."

Victor's gaze didn't leave the stone. "That was Dante for us."

Silence settled around them again. Birds chirped in a nearby tree, and for a moment, it felt like Dante was right there, laughing, running, calling out their names.

Victor exhaled, eyes closed. "I hope there will be good days for you, Dante," he whispered, brushing the stone once more. "Wherever you are."

They stood together in the golden hush of the evening, holding on to each other—and to the son they had lost, but would never let go.

* * * * *

Victor was locking up the bookshop when the phone rang. A number he hadn't seen in two months.

He picked it up. "Cyrus?"

On the other end, there were noises of heavy breathing. "He's back," Cyrus said, panting, the sound of crashing metal in the background. "Victor, listen to me, he's not a ghost anymore. The Imperium Nexus is active again. All the dormant trade routes, they've been lit. Smuggling lines, informant webs, weapon drops. Everything is back online. The Four Horsemen claims that you are one of them. The bounty on your head has been increased by him. Assassins all over London are looking for you."

Victor's blood turned to ice. "The four horsemen? Who's back?" he asked, though deep down, he already knew.

Cyrus whispered the name like a curse. "Valen Cross."

Victor stood motionless, the phone still pressed to his ear. Outside, the wind howled through Notting Hill, but inside, everything was still. He had then cut the call.

Vanessa walked in from the kitchen, drying her hands with a towel. "Who was it?" she asked.

Victor didn't answer immediately. He pulled out the chair, sat down slowly, exhaled as though a weight had returned to his chest. He looked up at her with steady eyes. "It was Cyrus," he said quietly. "The Imperium Nexus is back and Valen Cross is hunting me."

Vanessa froze. "Valen? It cannot be."

The underworld's brutal battle for ultimate power had reignited. This time, there would be no escape, no mercy. Every undercover criminal would be unveiled, every enemy hunted in by each other in a war that would consume them all. And in the shadows, a new force was rising. One that no one saw coming.

* * * * *